US

DUMB

AMERICANS

BY
C. L. POPE

AuthorHouse™
1663 Liberty Drive
Bloomington, IN 47403
www.authorhouse.com
Phone: 1-800-839-8640

First published by AuthorHouse   09/19/2011

ISBN: 978-1-4670-3795-2 (sc)
ISBN: 978-1-4670-3796-9 (ebk)

Printed in the United States of America

Any people depicted in stock imagery provided by Thinkstock are models, and such images are being used for illustrative purposes only.
Certain stock imagery © Thinkstock.

This book is printed on acid-free paper.

US

DUMB

AMERICANS

By

C. L. Pope

July

2011

FORWARD

The material in this book is written as seen though the eyes of an old 80 year old man, known by some

as 'THE OLD COOT..

From personal experience Clifford Pope has been an employee of two railroads -Santa Fe and the Burlington Northern as a damage merchandise adjuster and later as a Special Agent-FAA Controller and Flight Service Spec. and Facility Pilot, worked as a police officer-deputy sheriff and police chief. He owned and operated two hi-profile security and criminal investigation agencies and two insurance investigation agencies. Clifford Pope has an Associate of Science Degree in Law Enforcement.

I hope that young people who read this book that it will cause them to go to their parents and grandparents and ask them question about this book and their views on the US Government and other agencies.

I would like this book to be on eye opener for young people. especially those still in high school and cause them to realize what is in store for them when they finish high school and later retire

Material in this book is from my personal experience, my personal opinion and news articles about my subjects.

What I have talked about in this book is not even a drop in the bucket as to what the US Government is doing to the American Citizen.

COMON SENSE-SIMPLE SOLUTION: Cross party lines, Vote those old educated Idiots out of office.

FOR WHOM

After putting this book togather, I wish I could have said something nice about our Congresspeople and shown respect for them.

I first wrote and put this book togather for my Great Great Grandchildren to be able to compare my time to their time in life, I did not know anything about writting or how to put a book togather or how to have it Copyrights, but after some people saw the book, they told me I should have it published. God forbid if my old english teacher saw this book as I was her worst student.

The 70's 80's and 90's produced great inventions, jobs and wealth for young people and I'am sure if the government has not raised the taxes to 95% that my Great Great Grandchildren will see and experience new invention and a better life to come during their life time.

I only wish I could get the attention of our highschool and college students to inform them of what the Congresspeople have in store for them and what they are doing to the American Citizen. Some do listen and Riot and few are doing the job of the older American's who set back and complains and then votes the same Old Congresspeople back into office, Saying "I am only one person, What can I do?"

US
DUMB
AMERICANS

INDEX

I left space at the bottom of each subject so the reader can insert his / her opinion if they choose to do so.

US

DUMB

AMERICANS

By
C. L. Pope

HOW TRUE-HOW TRUE

HAS THE AMERICAN PEOPLE WOKE UP?

How many times have you seen your congressman hold so many Public Forum's? "NEVER" only when the American Public gets so outrage and protest and when the congressman is afraid of loosing the next election.

Has America finally woke up and become interested in out government as to what our Great Leaders have created in Washington.
I AM STILL WONDERING

LIES TO THE AMERICAN PUBLIC

STIMULUS HEAD START

Pay raises were counted as jobs 'saved,' review finds

WASHINGTON — The government's latest count of stimulus jobs overstates the effects of the $787 billion program under a federal preschool program, raising fresh questions about the process the Obama administration is using to tout the success of its economic recovery plan. An Associated Press review of the latest stimulus reports found that more than two-thirds of 14,506 jobs credited to the recovery act under spending by just one federal office were overstated because they counted pay increases for existing workers as jobs saved.

BISINESS AS USUAL

ANOTHER PRIME EXAMPLE OF COLLEGE EDUCATED C.E.O. IDIOTS LIEING TO THE AMERICAN PUBLIC.

NOTE IN THE ARTICLE BELOW THAT THE OWNERS CEO,s NAME OF NEW ORLEANS-BASED ENTERGY CORP. WAS LEFT OUT OF THE BELOW ARTICLE.

HOW MANY NUCLEAR REACTOR ACCIDENTS HAVE TO HAPPEN BEFORE THE AMERICAN PUBLIC SAYS 'NO MORE'?

Carcinogen taints at least 27 nuclear reactors
MONTPELIER, Vt. — Radioactive tritium, a carcinogen discovered in potentially dangerous levels in groundwater at the Vermont Yankee nuclear plant, has now tainted at least 27 of the nation's 104 nuclear reactors, raising concerns about how it is escaping from the aging nuclear plants. The leaks, many from deteriorating underground pipes, come as the nuclear industry is seeking and obtaining federal license renewals. New Orleans-based Entergy Corp., the plant's owner, has admitted misleading state regulators by denying that the plant had underground pipes that could leak tritium. No tritium has been found in area drinking water, the plant has said.
— *The Associated Press*

AND THEY KEEP TELLING US THAT NUCLEAR POWER PLANTS ARE SAFE

BRIEFLY

NRC investigates Comanche Peak
The Nuclear Regulatory Commission said Monday that it has begun a special inspection of the Comanche Peak nuclear generating plant in Glen Rose to determine why a backup generator failed during a test Nov. 21. The generator provides electricity to safety systems and components during a power loss. Dallas-based Luminant, the power-generating operation of the former TXU Corp., determined that painting done in the room housing the generator may have contributed to the failure, the NRC said. The agency said it expects two inspectors to spend several days at Comanche Peak and to file a written report within 30 to 45 days.
— *Jim Fuquay*

    If a test had not been run and there had been an emergenc
and the plant blew. Where would Cleburn and Burleson be today a
most of the Ft Worth/Dallas area because the wind on Nov. 21 w
from the south untill 8 am when the cold front came thru and
switched the wind to the south then Waco would have been in
trouble.

NCR, Tell me again that Nuclear Power Plants are safe.

US DUMB AMERICANS

Year 2009, American is in a Great Depression, the Dumb American public lets our Mayors-Companies-Corp.-Banks go up on the price of their products and interest. This is what Us Dumb Americans deserve by voting the same crooked congress people back into office and having a President and Congress that lets this happen.

H1N1

We Dumb Americans let our Government and Science in Atlanta stay in office after not telling the American people how bad the virus is from day one. Only one company in America makes the medicine and four from other countries make the Medicine.

What would happen if those four kept the medicine for themselves?

ILLEGALS

The U.S. Government lets Illegal's, Gang and Drug Dealers run wild. The government put some in jail causing a great debt to our economy and than turns them loose instead of sending them back South., The army that is stationed on the border can only report them as the come across the border but cannot stop them. Border Patrol can stop them any time within 8 miles of the border for any reason, but, further into the US they cannot be stopped except for traffic offence or a crime and they cannot be ask for citizenship papers.

Now our President wants to give all Illegal's a free pass, So, Why not do away with the Immigration Service which would lower the National Budget. Is this the story I heard about where the US lets all the Mexicans come into the US and after they are all here the US military movers into Mexico and takes over Mexico with out firing a shot? Than the Immigration Service could take over and run Mexico like a US State.

Thanks to our past and present Presidents and our good Congress People.

Tuesday, November 16, 2010

Court OKs in-state tuition for many illegal immigrants
CALIFORNIA — Illegal immigrants who graduated from California high schools can continue to receive lower, in-state tuition at the state's public universities and colleges, the California Supreme Court decided Monday. The ruling is the first of its kind in the nation. "Throughout the country, the California court decision will have reverberations," said Daniel Hurley, director of state relations and policy analysis for the American Association of State Colleges. He predicted that it would discourage challenges to similar policies in other states.
— Los Angeles Times

U.S. agrees to allow Mexican trucks

❯ Fifty percent of retaliatory tariffs would be lifted immediately.

By Tim Johnson
McClatchy Newspapers

MEXICO CITY — Mexico and the United States agreed in principle Thursday to open U.S. highways to Mexican long-haul trucks, ending a lingering safety dispute that prompted Mexico to impose more than $2 billion in retaliatory tariffs on U.S. exporters.

"After nearly 20 years, we finally have found a clear path to resolving the dispute over trucking between our two countries," President Barack Obama said at a White House news conference with Mexican President Felipe Calderon at his side.

The agreement calls for Mexico to lift 50 percent of its retaliatory tariffs immediately while Mexican truckers undergo safety, language and driver training.

Obama said he will move ahead "in a way that strengthens the safety of cross-border trucking, lifts tariffs on billions of dollars of U.S. goods, expands our exports to Mexico and creates jobs on both sides of the border."

But Teamsters union President Jim Hoffa charged that the agree-

Mexican President Felipe Calderon and President Barack Obama announced the agreement Thursday. The Teamsters union opposes the move, saying Mexican trucks aren't as safe.
The Associated Press/Charles Dharapak

ment "caves in to business interests," adding that "Mexican trucks simply don't meet the same standards as U.S. trucks."

And a group representing 152,000 independent truckers said the agreement will make their struggle to survive a sour economy even more difficult.

"Simply unbelievable," Todd Spencer, executive vice president of the Owner-Operator Independent Drivers Association, said in a statement. "For all the president's talk of helping small businesses survive, his administration is sure doing their best to destroy small trucking companies and the drivers they employ."

The 1994 North American Free Trade Agree-

ment that binds Mexico, the United States and Canada authorized U.S. and Mexican carriers to cross the border. But Washington imposed a ban after the Teamsters union and its allies in Congress said Mexican trucks were unsafe. Mexico later won a NAFTA dispute settlement saying the ban violated the treaty, but it didn't impose retaliatory tariffs until 2009.

The U.S. Chamber of Commerce and the American Trucking Association praised Thursday's move, while the Teamsters said an accord would bring danger to U.S. highways.

"It is long past time for the United States to live up to its trade commitment and allow cross-border trucking services.

This delay put more than 25,000 jobs at risk," the chamber's president, Thomas J. Donohue, said in a statement.

A trucking agreement would end "job-killing tariffs" by Mexico, he added, and offer "certainty to trucking companies and shippers throughout North America."

Hoffa, however, said the accord wouldn't benefit U.S. trucking companies.

"Given the drug violence, there's no way a U.S. company would want to haul valuable goods into the Mexican interior," Hoffa said.

A White House statement said the two nations agreed on "a phased-in program built on the highest safety standards." Once a final agreement is reached, Mexico will reduce punitive tariffs by 50 percent, removing the remaining 50 percent when the first Mexican truck is granted permission to enter the U.S.

Mexican truckers must abide by U.S. motor-safety standards, undergo periodic screening for illegal drug use and comply with U.S. rules on how many hours a day they can drive.

The agreement will require approval from Congress.

17

Customs agents spotting, not stopping stolen vehicles

System on Mexico border identifies suspicious tags

The New York Times

SAN DIEGO -- As many as 2,000 stolen vehicles pass by the San Diego border station on their way into Mexico each year, customs officials say.

How do they know? They have a machine that beeps whenever a stolen license plate goes by.

Why do customs officials not stop the cars?

"It would be great if we could do that," said Dennis Murphy, a spokesman for the U.S. Customs Service, which installed the license plate readers at 11 of its 31 Southwest border crossings over the past two years. The main reason for installing the machines, which cost $63,000 each, was to record vehicles leaving and entering the country for possible criminal investigations. Stopping stolen cars was another goal.

Because customs officers inspect only those cars entering the country, "It's not like we can just throw ourselves in front of every stolen car we see and say, 'Stop,'" Murphy said.

But in the two years since customs officials set up the machines, they have not coordinated with local police agencies to stop stolen cars leaving the country, except for one pilot program in Arizona. And many machines have been installed so close to the border that it would be difficult to stop drivers before they leave the country.

At the San Ysidro border crossing near San Diego, four plate readers are set up in each lane of the freeway about 500 feet from the Mexican border. They scan cars heading south, quickly run the license number through an FBI database and set off a high-pitched alarm whenever they hit on a plate that has been reported stolen.

Inside the nearby customs office, inspectors barely look up anymore when they hear the sound. "What's the point?" said one. "We're not going to do anything about it anyway."

The beeping plate reader, which goes off from four to eight times a day, has been a source of frustration since it showed up.

"We were told it was going to be part of a federal-local task force that would nab the stolen vehicles before they got into Mexico," said a retired inspector who was a supervisor at San Ysidro when the machine arrived. "Nothing ever happened."

For today's Star-Telegram and more news and features, go to www.star-telegram.com To search the metroplex, go to www.dfw.com

Inspectors, he said, constantly complained about the futility of having to watch what they considered a "crime wave" of car theft -- a daily parade that would add up to more than 2,000 vehicles a year heading south. With the typical stolen car worth about $13,300, according to the California Highway Patrol, that would mean an annual loss of more than $26 million.

The five U.S. cities with the highest auto theft rates -- Los Angeles, Phoenix, Houston, San Diego and Riverside, Calif. -- are within a few hundred miles of the border. In 1998, the crime bureau said, 161,499 cars were reported stolen from those cities.

Customs officials say help may be on the way from a new customs financing bill that proposes enough money to send 1,754 new employees and $151 million worth of high-tech equipment to the Southwest border. Included would be money for more plate readers, but customs was not able to offer a timetable for when the technology would be used to stop stolen cars.

Citizenship: Congress has remedy for illegal immigration

IMMIGRATION

CITIZENSHIP A BIRTHRIGHT? MAYBE NOT

A misinterpretation of the 14th Amendment has led to the greatest possible inducement for illegal entry to the United States.

A simple reform would drain some scalding steam from immigration arguments that may soon again be at a roiling boil. It would bring the interpretation of the 14th Amendment into conformity with what the authors intended, and with common sense, thereby removing an incentive for illegal immigration.

To end the practice of "birthright citizenship," all that is required is to correct the misinterpretation of that amendment's first sentence: "All persons born or naturalized in the United States, and subject to the jurisdiction thereof, are citizens of the United States and of the state wherein they reside." From these words has flowed the practice of conferring citizenship on children born here to illegal immigrants.

Professor Lino Graglia of the University of Texas law school writes that a parent from a poor country "can hardly do more for a child than make him or her an American citizen, entitled to all the advantages of the American welfare state." Therefore, "It is difficult to imagine a more irrational and self-defeating legal system than one which makes unauthorized entry into this country a criminal offense and simultaneously provides perhaps the greatest possible inducement to illegal entry."

Writing in the *Texas Review of Law and Politics*, Graglia says this irrationality is rooted in a misunderstanding of the phrase "subject to the jurisdiction thereof." What was this intended or understood to mean by those who wrote it in 1866 and ratified it in 1868? The authors and ratifiers could not have intended birthright citizenship for illegal immigrants, because in 1868 *there were and never had been any illegal immigrants* because *no law ever had restricted immigration.*

GEORGE WILL

If those who wrote and ratified the 14th Amendment *had* imagined laws restricting immigration, and had anticipated huge waves of illegal immigration, is it reasonable to presume that they would have wanted to provide the reward of citizenship to the children of the violators of those laws? Surely not.

The Civil Rights Act of 1866 begins with language from which the 14th Amendment's Citizenship Clause is derived: "All persons born in the United States, *and not subject to any foreign power*, excluding Indians not taxed, are hereby declared to be citizens of the United States." (Emphasis added.) The explicit exclusion of Indians from birthright citizenship was not repeated in the 14th Amendment because it was considered unnecessary. Although Indians were at least partially subject to U.S. jurisdiction, they owed allegiance to their tribes, not the United States. This reasoning — divided allegiance — applies equally to exclude the children of resident aliens, legal as well as illegal, from birthright citizenship.

Indeed, today's regulations issued by the departments of Homeland Security and Justice stipulate: "A person born in the United States to a foreign diplomatic officer accredited to the United States, as a matter of international law, is not subject to the jurisdiction of the United States. That person is not a United States citizen under the 14th Amendment."

Sen. Lyman Trumbull of Illinois was, Graglia writes, one of two "principal authors of the citizenship clauses in 1866 act and the 14th Amendment." He said "subject to the jurisdiction of the United States" meant subject to its "complete" jurisdiction, meaning "not owing allegiance to anybody else." Hence, children whose Indian parents had tribal allegiances were excluded from birthright citizenship.

Appropriately, in 1884 the Supreme Court held that children born to Indian parents were not born "subject to" U.S. jurisdiction because, among other reasons, the person so born could not change his status by his "own will without the action or assent of the United States." And "no one can become a citizen of a nation without its consent." Graglia says this decision "seemed to establish" that U.S. citizenship is "a consensual relation, requiring the consent of the United States." So: "This would clearly settle the question of birthright citizenship for children of illegal aliens. There cannot be a more total or forceful denial of consent to a person's citizenship than to make the source of that person's presence in the nation illegal."

Congress has heard testimony estimating that more than two-thirds of all births in Los Angeles public hospitals, more than half of all births in that city and nearly 10 percent of all births in the nation in recent years have been to illegal immigrant mothers. Graglia seems to establish that there is no constitutional impediment to Congress ending the granting of birthright citizenship to people whose presence here is "not only without the government's consent but in violation of its law."

GEORGE WILL WRITES FOR THE WASHINGTON POST WRITERS GROUP.
GEORGEWILL@WASHPOST.COM

Feds move to relax rules for deportation

> Obama administration plans to deport convicted felons only.

By Susan Carroll
Houston Chronicle

The Homeland Security Department is systematically reviewing thousands of pending immigration cases and moving to dismiss those filed against suspected illegal immigrants who have no felony convictions, according to several sources familiar with the efforts.

Culling the immigration court system dockets of nonfelons started in earnest in Houston about a month ago and has stunned local immigration attorneys, who have reported going to court anticipating clients' deportations only to learn that the government was dismissing their cases.

Richard Rocha, an Immigration and Customs Enforcement spokesman, said Tuesday that the review is part of a broader, nationwide strategy to prioritize the deportations of illegal immigrants who pose a threat to national security and public safety.

Critics assailed the plan as another sign that the Obama administration is trying to create a kind of backdoor "amnesty" program.

Raed Gonzalez, an immigration attorney who was briefed on the effort by Homeland Security's deputy chief counsel in Houston, said the department confirmed that it's reviewing cases nationwide, though not yet to the pace of the local office. He said the others are expected to follow suit soon.

Gonzalez, the liaison between the Executive Office for Immigration Review, which administers the immigration court system, and the American Immigration Lawyers Association, said Homeland Security now has five attorneys assigned to reviewing cases in Houston's immigration court.

Gonzalez said the attorneys are conducting the reviews case by case. However, he said, they are following general guidelines that allow for the dismissal of cases for defendants who have been in the country for two or more years and have no felony convictions.

Opponents of illegal immigration were critical of the dismissals.

"They've made clear that they have no interest in enforcing immigration laws against people who are not convicted criminals," said Mark Krikorian, executive director of the Center for Immigration Studies, which advocates for strict controls.

"This situation is just another side effect of President Obama's failure to deliver on his campaign promise to make immigration reform a priority in his first year," said U.S. Sen. John Cornyn, R-Texas.

Gonzalez called the dismissals necessary step in unclogging a massive backlog.

N. Texas lawmakers seek more border troops

By Anna M. Tinsley
atinsley@star-telegram.com

Several North Texas congressional members are calling on President Barack Obama to help secure the Texas-Mexico border by sending more troops.

They are echoing a call by Gov. Rick Perry, who first asked the president for 1,000 National Guard troops in February 2009. And while members of Congress are glad that 250 Guard troops were sent to the border Aug. 1, they say it's not enough.

"Although the response was appreciated, it is woefully inadequate," said the letter to Obama, which includes the signatures of Republican U.S. Reps. Michael Burgess of Lewisville, Joe Barton of Arlington, Kay

Granger

Granger of Fort Worth and Kenny Marchant of Coppell. "Violence along the border is on the rise and we must face this problem head-on with the proper equipment and manpower needed to protect American citizens.

"We would appreciate your timely response in justifying your initial offer of 250 troops, and urge you to expeditiously authorize the remaining 750 troops necessary to patrol the largest border of any southern state."

Obama's administration sent 1,200 Guard troops to the four states bordering Mexico. Perry has repeatedly asked for more and gave Obama staffers a letter repeating his request when the president attended fundraisers this month in Texas.

When asked about the congressional letter, federal officials referred to an Aug. 4 letter to Perry from Homeland Security Secretary Janet Napolitano.

"Over the past year and a half, DHS has dedicated historic levels of personnel, technology, and resources to the Southwest border," the letter said.

"Today, the Border Patrol is better staffed than at any time in its 86-year history, having nearly doubled the number of agents from approximately 10,000 in 2004 to more than 20,000 today."

Anna M. Tinsley. 817-390-7610

THESE TWO ARTICLES SHOW WHY OUR COUNTRY IS IN SUCH A MESS. WHY DON'T THE U.S. JUST TAKE OVER MEXICO?

Few firms fined for hiring illegal immigrants

> Records show that the U.S. has often failed to punish companies.

By Susan Carroll
Houston Chronicle

Immigration inspectors poring over the hiring paperwork of a California company last summer found that 262 employees -- a whopping 93 percent of the work force – had "suspect" documents on file.

At an Illinois service company, auditors found dubious documents for nearly 8 in 10 of the 200-plus employees.

Inspectors examining records at a Texas manufacturing firm found suspicious paperwork for more than half of the 107 employees.

But the companies didn't pay a penny in fines. No employers were led away in handcuffs. Immigration and Customs Enforcement officials didn't even issue them a formal warning, the agency's internal records show.

Instead, they were instructed to purge their payrolls of illegal immigrants. Armed with assurances that the workers with suspect documents were fired – or, in the Texas case, "self-terminated" -- the ICE auditors closed the cases.

The cases are a few examples included in ICE's internal records on its audit initiative, an enforcement program launched in July 2009 by the Obama administration officials.

ICE had faced criticism for raiding job sites and rounding up large numbers of illegal immigrants for deportation but not necessarily building cases against employers. With the audit initiative, ICE aims to scrutinize the hiring records of more businesses and impose what top officials describe as "tough" and "smart" employer sanctions.

But ICE audit records obtained recently through a Freedom of Information Act request show that the agency has, in many instances, failed to punish companies found to have significant numbers or high percentages of workers with questionable documents. In response to the records request, ICE provided limited details on about 430 audit cases it had listed as "closed" through February.

The records show inspectors identified more than 110 companies with suspect documents, with nearly half having questionable paperwork for 10 or more workers.

In total, the agency ordered 14 companies to pay fines totaling nearly $150,000, but noted no employer arrests in connection with the cases.

ICE officials say the audits and the broader strategy of aggressively pursuing employers are getting results.

Brett Dreyer, the head of ICE's work site enforcement unit, said that ICE tries to determine which employers may have been duped into unintentionally accepting fraudulent documents from employees and which ones are "turning a blind eye" to workers' legal status.

THE WILL OF THE AMERICAN PEOPLE DOES NOT EXIST IN THE U.S.A.

Texas' Hispanic-owned businesses blossoming

> Business growth has followed population growth, but there are other factors.

By Scott Nishimura
snishimura@star-telegram.com

Texas was among the nation's leaders in Hispanic-owned businesses in 2007, with the second-largest number of firms, the top

---

By the numbers: Texas and Hispanic-owned businesses. 4C

---

three cities and three of the five leading counties, the U.S. Census said Tuesday.

But there's work to be done: Only 44,000 Hispanic-owned firms nationally had gross receipts of at least $1 million.

In Tarrant County, 18,582 Hispanic-owned businesses made up 11.7 percent of all businesses but accounted for only 1.6 percent of sales, according to the data in the Census Bureau's latest survey of business ownership, which is conducted every five years.

"We see a community that continues to grow, yet the true economic potential has yet to be fully realized," said David Hinson, national director of the Commerce Department's Minority Business Development Agency.

Texas had 447,486 Hispanic-owned businesses, up 40 percent from 319,340 in the 2002 survey. It trailed only California.

An estimated 21 percent of Texas firms were Hispanic-owned, trailing New Mexico and Florida.

Hidalgo and El Paso counties ranked No. 1 and No. 2 among U.S. counties for Hispanic-

More on HISPANICS, 4C

owned businesses as a percent of all businesses. Bexar County was No. 5. El Paso, San Antonio and Houston were the top three U.S. cities for the percentage of Hispanic-owned businesses.

Business growth has followed Hispanic population growth, but there are other factors, Hinson said.

"There's been a true maturing of the Hispanic community related to entrepreneurism," he said. "You're having more and more young people look at that option as opposed to merely looking for a job."

Hispanic business ownership is concentrated in key segments. Wholesale and retail trade and construction accounted for 51 percent of all Hispanic business revenue in 2007. In Tarrant County, construction, wholesale trade and manufacturing made up 56 percent.

In Texas, Hispanic-owned businesses generated $62.1 billion in 2007 sales, 2.3 percent of the $2.6 trillion generated by all firms. In the 2002 survey, Hispanic businesses in Texas had $42.2 billion in sales.

The county's Hispanic-owned businesses had revenue of $2.9 billion in 2007, compared with $174.7 billion generated by all businesses.

"That says we have a lot of very small businesses," said Vince Puente, co-owner of Southwest Office Systems, a Tarrant County firm founded by his father in 1964. "It just leaves plenty of room for the Hispanic business owner to grow."

NEXT PAGE

22

Texas stands out

States with largest percentage of Hispanic-owned firms

State	2007 Hispanic firms	% of all firms
New Mexico	37,155	24
Florida	450,185	22
Texas	447,486	21
California	565,567	17
Arizona	52,667	11

Counties with largest percentage of Hispanic-owned firms

Hidalgo, Texas	45,016	69
El Paso, Texas	38,791	61
Miami-Dade, Fla.	244,348	60
Bronx, N.Y.	41,811	38
Bexar, Texas	49,526	37

Cities with largest percentage of Hispanic-owned firms*

El Paso	31,640	60
San Antonio	43,081	39
Houston	51,207	23
Albuquerque	10,284	23
Los Angeles	94,629	21

* Cities with 500,000 or more population.

Source: U.S. Census, 2007 Survey of Business Owners

Who's in charge

Mexicans and Mexican-Americans owned most Hispanic businesses in Texas and Tarrant County in 2007.

Texas

Hispanic firms	447,486
Mexican/Mexican-American	356,706

Tarrant County

Hispanic firms	18,582
Mexican/Mexican-American	14,127

Source: U.S. Census, 2007 Survey of Business Owners

The number of Texas Hispanic firms with employees grew to 41,321 in 2007 from 34,399 in 2002. Total employment at Hispanic firms rose to 398,152 from 280,156.

Tarrant County had 1,470 firms with employees in 2007, and total employees were 18,628. The Census Bureau did not publish comparable figures for Tarrant County in 2002.

Robert Fernandez, a certified public accountant in Fort Worth who opened his own firm in 1987, after several years working for two of the big accounting and audit firms, said the overall numbers are encouraging.

The numbers show "we are contributing more to the financial success of the community, as opposed to just sitting back and collecting a paycheck," he said. "We're able to demonstrate we can get firms successfully established."

He wants to see better distribution of Hispanic firms. Specifically, he wants more competition than the three or four Hispanic-owned accounting firms he estimates are in Fort Worth.

Rosa Navejar, president of the Fort Worth Hispanic Chamber of Commerce, was encouraged by the presence of Hispanic-owned businesses in the professional, scientific and technical category, where the bureau estimated 1,169 Tarrant County firms.

"When I was growing up, the Hispanic businesses were restaurants," she said. "Now you see Hispanic businesses in construction and professional services."

She sees more Hispanic women go into business as a way to maintain flexibility at home. "Single mothers can dictate their own schedule," she said.

Navejar said she's also seeing a gradual spread of Hispanic-owned businesses across the county, instead of locating in traditional areas. She remembers several years ago counseling one man seeking to open a Mexican restaurant to consider locations besides the north side.

The man opened in Haltom City close to Loop 820 instead and is doing well, she said.

"If he'd opened up on the north side, he probably would have failed," Navejar said.

What has happened to Hispanic business owners since 2007?

"The business community has probably taken a hit just like any others," Fernandez said. "But I don't see a lessening of interest in starting your own business. If people have lost jobs, they might be starting other businesses to get a paycheck."

Puente knows one such story, a man who worked for a fence-building company who lost his job during the recession. "Now he's out there doing his own jobs," Puente said.

Scott Nishimura, 817-390-7808

Obama to Latinos: 'Don't forget who is standing with you'

◙ The president pledges to keep working for immigration reform.

By Darlene Superville
The Associated Press

WASHINGTON — President Barack Obama appealed to Hispanics on Wednesday to support Democrats in the November elections despite his failed promise to pass an immigration overhaul.

"Don't forget who is standing with you," the president said as he blamed Republicans for standing in the way of progress.

Less than two months before midterm elections that could prove disastrous for Democrats who run Congress, Obama acknowledged the disappointment among Latinos over the immigration issue and pledged to keep pushing for a comprehensive overhaul of the nation's immigration laws to deal with border security and provide an eventual route to legal status for the estimated 11 million illegal immigrants in the United States.

"You have every right to keep the heat on me and the Democrats, and I hope you do. That's how our political process works," Obama said the Congressional Hispanic Caucus Institute's awards dinner. "But don't forget who is standing with you, and who is standing against you. Don't ever believe that this election coming up doesn't matter. "

Obama also promised to help win passage of a bill, known as the DREAM Act, that would allow young people who attend college or join the military to become legal U.S. residents.

Obama cast Republicans as the bad guys in the tussle over immigration, saying some GOP senators who in the past had supported a comprehensive approach now oppose moving forward just to thwart his agenda.

"Now I know that many of you campaigned hard for me, and understandably you're frustrated that we have not been able to move this over the finish line yet. I am too," he said. "But let me be clear: I will not walk away from this fight. My commitment is to getting this done as soon as we can."

Some in the audience shouted "When?"

Obama urged Hispanics to remember who extended healthcare to millions of children, provided Pell Grants for Latino students, enacted credit card reform and created an agency to protect consumers from predatory lending, including millions of immigrants who send money to relatives in their native countries.

"Don't forget who your friends are," he said. "No se olviden" — Spanish for "Don't forget."

Obama's message Is "All You Latinos Get Into America As Soon As You Can Anyway You Can"

24

Failure of sanctuary cities bill spurs GOP infighting

❯ They blame one another for the death of the Perry priority bill.

By Jim Vertuno
The Associated Press

AUSTIN — When the Texas Legislature's special session began, Republican majorities in the House and Senate warned Democrats that they wouldn't be able to stop an immigration enforcement bill that had sparked one of the toughest fights of the year.

The bill would have given police more power to ask anyone they detain about their citizenship status, a measure Hispanic Democrats derided as racist and a tool to harass Latinos.

But when the bill died again this week without a vote in the House, Democrats smirked while Gov. Rick Perry and GOP lawmakers angrily blamed one another for its demise.

Lt. Gov. David Dewhurst and the Senate blamed the House. The House blamed the Senate.

Perry chimed in, picking on Sen. Robert Duncan and prompting colleagues of the Lubbock lawmaker to rally around him.

Ultimately, the Republican majorities in both chambers left one of Perry's priority issues for dead and ended the session Wednesday taking aim at in a circular firing squad.

The Senate "failed," House Speaker Joe Straus said.

Dewhurst tweaked the House by noting that twice in the previous week the House failed to get 100 members needed to show up to do work.

House Republican leader Larry Phillips of Friendswood had gone to the Bahamas on vacation with his family. Dewhurst noted he canceled a trip to France for D-Day invasion anniversary celebrations to stay in Austin.

A Perry priority

Perry, who is considering a run for president, made the so-called sanctuary cities bill one of his priorities during the regular session and put it on the agenda of the special session.

Perry and supporters say the bill would have helped police fight crime committed by illegal immigrants. But opponents, including many police chiefs and sheriffs, said it would allow rogue officers to target Latinos.

Republicans in both chambers had the muscle to pass any bill they wanted during the regular session if they used it.

The Senate, where Democrats were able to block the bill during the regular session, passed the immigration bill June 15 after several hours of tense, emotional debate.

That sent the bill to the House, where the Republicans hold a 101-49 supermajority big enough to pass bills whether Democrats even bothered to show up to vote.

The House had passed the bill by a wide margin during the regular session

and was expected to do so again. But this time, the House let the bill languish and die in committee.

Perry and House Republicans tried to negotiate a version of the immigration bill into a must-pass budget bill that included $4 billion in public education cuts. The theory was that because the immigration bill potentially withholds state grant money from law enforcement agencies if they did not comply, the budget bill was an appropriate place to put it.

That's where Duncan came in. As the lead negotiator on the budget bill, Perry blamed him for standing in the way and the Senate refused to add the immigration provision.

The Senate Republican Caucus told Perry to back off.

Caucus Chairman Sen. Robert Nichols of Jacksonville said the group considered the change but told Duncan no for fear it would jeopardize the entire budget bill.

The House had its chance to pass the Senate version on its own, Nichols said.

Democrats thankful

Democrats, meanwhile, watched the bill die without having to do anything to kill it.

"Latino citizens who faced racial profiling and discrimination under this bill can breathe a sigh of relief," said Sen. Carlos Uresti, D-San Antonio, chairman of the Senate Hispanic Caucus.

In other word this DUMB AMERICAN understands the above that REPUBLICANS are saying all of U'all Illegals come on to Texas and U'all Illegals that are here can stay.

U.S. won't give Texas more troops for the Mexican border

▶ The state can call up guardsmen at its own expense, an official says.

By Stewart M. Powell
Houston Chronicle

WASHINGTON — Homeland Security Secretary Janet Napolitano on Friday rebuffed Gov. Rick Perry's calls for more federally paid National Guard troops to combat threatened spillover violence along

Napolitano

the Mexican border, saying that federal law enforcement is adequate and that governors can call up National Guard troops at state expense anytime.

Napolitano's comments were the latest in politically charged exchanges between Perry, a Republican, and the Obama administration, dating to Perry's call for 1,000 federally paid National Guard troops 20 months ago.

President Barack Obama ordered 250 National Guard troops to the border at federal expense in August as part of an emergency call-up of 1,200 troops for duty along the U.S.-Mexico border.

But the administration has resisted calls for additional troops, citing a $600 million buildup of federal law enforcement personnel and technology in response to Mexican drug wars that have claimed more than 28,000 lives in Mexico in four years.

"We have been putting resources into the border at an unprecedented rate," Napolitano said at a luncheon with reporters. "Ci-

vilian law enforcement is being plussed up all along the border."

Among the additional border security measures, Napolitano also cited deployment of an unmanned Predator aircraft based in Corpus Christi. It provides aerial surveillance along the eastern part of the Mexican border to match surveillance along the western sector provided by an Arizona-based Predator.

The Obama administration is "paying particular attention" to border communities concerned about spillover violence, Napolitano said.

But neither Customs and Border Protection, the Homeland Security agency that oversees the U.S. Border Patrol, nor local county sheriffs see any sign of drug war violence threatening U.S. border communities, as some Republican politicians claim, Napolitano said.

Perry "always has the ability in a way to bring up National Guard if he's going to pay for them," said Napolitano, a former governor of Arizona.

"That's always an option available to a governor."

Perry has criticized the Obama administration for allocating Texas only 20 percent of the federally paid National Guard troops along the southwest border when the state's border accounts for 64 percent of the 1,969-mile border.

Perry spokeswoman Katherine Cesinger said Friday that border and homeland security remain "federal responsibilities.

"As a former border governor, Secretary Napolitano knows how greatly unjust it is for this administration to pass the cost and burden of keeping the entire nation safe on to the taxpayers of Texas," Cesinger said.

Obama wants all Mexicans to come into the U.S. than the U.S. can take over Mexico with out firing a shot

26

President revives his campaign for immigration overhaul

> Latinos are growing increasingly frustrated with his policies.

By Julia Preston
The New York Times

President Barack Obama told a gathering of business, labor, religious and political leaders at the White House on Tuesday that he remains committed to an overhaul of the nation's immigration laws and wants to try again in the coming months to push Congress to pass a bill.

With his re-election campaign launched this month and Latino communities growing increasingly frustrated with his immigration policies, Obama summoned more than 60 high-profile supporters of the stalled overhaul legislation to a strategy session, looking for ways to revive it. Among those attending were Mayor Michael Bloomberg of New York, an independent; Mayor Julian Castro of San Antonio, a Democrat; and former Gov. Arnold Schwarzenegger of California, a Republican.

Two big-city police chiefs, Raymond Kelly of New York and Charles Ramsey of Philadelphia, were there, as was Sheryl Sandberg, a top executive at Facebook, and Leith Anderson, president of the National Association of Evangelicals, the largest group of evangelical Christians.

Prospects for the proposed policy, which would grant legal status to millions of illegal immigrants and revamp the immigration system, seem bleak in this Congress, with staunch Republican opponents of the bill controlling pivotal committee positions in the House. Recently Latino leaders have stepped up their criticism of Obama, as deportations have reached record numbers under his administration and he has offered no relief from the crackdown on immigrant communities.

Latino voters helped several Democrats, including Sen. Harry Reid of Nevada, the majority leader, survive the Republican shift in the midterm elections last fall, and they are expected to be a major force next year.

In the closed meeting, Obama argued that the overhaul would bring immigrant entrepreneurs to the United States and was a crucial piece of the economic recovery, according to several people who attended. He sought views on whether to try to pass smaller pieces of the massive overhaul, such as a bill that would give legal status to illegal immigrant students, or one that would increase visas for highly skilled foreign workers.

The president asked for help to "change the debate" to attract Republicans to support the bill. He said he could not pass the overhaul "if I am leading the debate alone," according to a White House statement.

Bloomberg suggested recasting the acrimonious discussion over the proposed policy to stress that it would not take jobs from Americans but would help the economy, said John Feinblatt, the chief policy adviser to the mayor.

Obama is asked to delay deportations

WASHINGTON — Twenty-two Senate Democrats are pressuring President Barack Obama to delay deportations of certain young immigrants in the U.S. illegally.

The senators ask in a letter for deferrals of any deportations of the young immigrants brought to the U.S. by parents who arrived or stayed illegally.

The senators also suggest smaller steps the president can take to help the young immigrants, such as making sure they know they can request deportation delays.

In the letter sent Wednesday, the senators acknowledge that Obama must enforce the law but say exercising prosecutorial discretion has a long history in the U.S. and is consistent with the rule of law.

Last year, the House passed the DREAM Act, which would have allowed the youths to stay in the U.S., but it failed in the Senate.

— The Associated Press

Schools reminded they can't turn away illegal immigrants

◘ The Supreme Court has upheld all students' right to public education.

By Christine Armario
The Associated Press

MIAMI — The U.S. Department of Education sent a letter to districts around the country Friday, reminding them that all students — legal or not — are entitled to a public education.

The letter comes amid reports that schools may be checking the immigration status of students trying to enroll and reminds districts they are federally prohibited from barring elementary or secondary students on the basis of citizenship status.

"Moreover, districts may not request information with the purpose or result of denying access to public schools on the basis of race, color or national origin," said the letter, which was signed by officials from the department's Office of Civil Rights and the Department of Justice.

"We put this letter out now because we know school districts are in the process of planning for the next school year, and wanted to make sure they had this in hand," said Department of Education spokesman Justin Hamilton. "We were concerned about the number of reports that we've received and heard about, and felt it was necessary to make it clear that this has been the law of the land since Ronald Reagan was president."

A 1982 Supreme Court case, *Plyer v. Doe*, held that states cannot deny students access to public education, whether they are in the U.S. legally or not. The court ruled that denying public education could impose a lifetime of hardship "on a discrete class of children not accountable for their disabling status."

The letter comes as the Office of Civil Rights investigates three complaints, including one by the Southern Poverty Law center on behalf of a girl who was asked for her passport and visa when attempting to enroll in high school in Durham County, N.C.

Gerri Katzerman, an attorney with the Southern Poverty Law Center, said the issue has become increasingly common in the Deep South as demographics change.

"We hear from them a very similar experience, where they attempt to enroll and are asked about their immigration status, are asked for documents they don't have, and they basically disappear back into the population without having the opportunity to participate in public education," she said.

Mexico: Hub for Drug Flow

▶ MEXICO IS THE HUB FOR MANY DRUGS FROM many regions, and a complex network of routes carries the drugs north to the United States. Drug cartels (inset map) violently compete for their share of drug profits.

UNITED STATES

MEXICO

MEXICO CITY ★

☐ Disputed Territory
☒ Cartel Pacifico Sur
☐ La Familia Michoacana
☐ Sinaloa Federation
▥ Arellano Felix Organization
☐ Gulf Cartel
■ Carrillo Fuentes Organization
▨ Edgar Valdez Villarreal Faction
▦ Los Zetas

San Diego
Tijuana
Mexicali
Tucson
Nogales
Douglas
Agua Prieta
El Paso
Juarez

UNITED STATES

MEXICO

Ejido San Miguel
Nuevo Laredo
Laredo
McAllen
Reynosa

Gulf of Mexico

Culiacan

Mazatlan

Pacific Ocean

Tampico

Cocaine From Colombia, Venezuela, Brazil

Merida
Cancun

Puerto Vallarta

Veracruz

BELIZE

Ephedra From Asia

MEXICO CITY ★

GUATEMALA

Lazaro Cardenas

HONDURAS

Acapulco

Cocaine From Colombia

☐ Cocaine Traffic
▨ Ephedra Traffic
☐ Marijuana and Meth Traffic
■ All Drug Traffic

SOURCE: www.stratfor.com

Young illegal immigrants nationwide pushing government to let them stay

> Activists take a risk by publicly revealing their status.

By Kate Brumback
The Associated Press

ATLANTA — Eighteen-year-old Dulce Guerrero kept quiet about being an illegal immigrant until this year, when she became upset after a traffic stop that landed her mother in jail for two nights. The arrest came as Georgia lawmakers were crafting what would become one of the nation's toughest immigration crackdowns, and Guerrero feared her mother would be deported.

"I feel like that was my breaking point, when my mom was in jail," said Guerrero, a recent high school graduate who came to the U.S. from Mexico when she was 2. "I felt like, well, that's it, it can't get any worse than this. My mother has been to jail."

Guerrero first publicly announced her immigration status at a protest in March, and now she's organizing a rally under the tutelage of more experienced activists who are themselves only a few years older. The high-stakes movement of young illegal immigrants declaring that they're "undocumented and unafraid" got a boost this week when a Pulitzer Prize-winning journalist revealed he's been living in the country illegally.

Guerrero is the chief organizer of a rally set for Tuesday at the Georgia State Capitol for high school-age illegal immigrants to tell their stories. She and others hope to draw attention to the plight of the hundreds of thousands of young people who were brought to the U.S. illegally by their parents.

Already nationwide, efforts by young activists have ranged from rallies and letter writing to sit-ins and civil disobedience, drawing inspiration from civil rights demonstrations decades ago, with the aim of forcing the federal government to reform rules for immigrants in their situation.

In one of the most high-profile declarations yet, former *Washington Post* reporter Jose Antonio Vargas used an ABC News interview and a *New York Times Magazine* article to announce Wednesday that he is an illegal immigrant from the Philippines.

"It's very exciting," said 25-year-old Mohammad Abdollahi, a veteran protester who's helping Guerrero. Vargas' revelation "shows that we exist in all walks of life. Folks don't realize how American we are," he said.

Those who come forward make themselves vulnerable, but it's no guarantee they'll have to leave the U.S. right away. Some have been deported despite broad support from their communities asking that they be allowed to stay. Others, like Georgia college student and cause celebre Jessica Colotl, have won at least temporary reprieves.

Mandeep Chahal, an honors student at the University of California, Davis, and her mother were granted a stay in their deportation proceedings Tuesday after Chahal, 20, campaigned on Facebook to avoid being sent back to India.

Proponents of stricter enforcement of immigration laws often concede that young people in this situation are among the most sympathetic cases but that legalizing them still raises problems.

I say let them all come to the U.S. and as soon as they are all here the U.S. can take over Mexico without firing a shot. "Us Dumb Americans" are going to let the President and Congress do as they please as they have done in the past 30 years. It is no wonder we do not have jobs for the working class, All the work is in China.

In Mansfield, fence separating cemeteries is painful reminder

Norman and Brenda Norwood, Elliott Lawson and McClendon Moody are among those with Mansfield ties who want the fence removed.
Star-Telegram/Paul Moseley

A fence between two 19th-century cemeteries in Mansfield has been in place so long, many residents may not think much of it or even notice it at all. That's not true of everyone, though. The fence was originally built to divide the "colored" cemetery and the Mansfield Cemetery, serving as a literal barrier for black citizens for many years. As Mansfield has grown, evolving into one of Tarrant County's biggest and most diverse cities, some black residents want the fence removed because, for them, it symbolizes a bygone era of separatism.
Chris Vaughn, 1B

The fence separates the "colored" cemetery, in background, from the Mansfield Cemetery. It has been there as long as anyone can remember.

The Black are just like the Illegal Wetback, Always have to complain about something.

34

Friday, July 15, 2011

California to require gay history curriculum

▶ Budget cuts will delay the curriculum materials until 2015.

By Josh Richman and Theresa Harrington
Contra Costa Times

WALNUT CREEK, Calif. — Public schools must incorporate the historical contributions of gays and lesbians into their lesson plans, under a law signed Thursday by Gov. Jerry Brown.

SB48, the FAIR (Fair, Accurate, Inclusive and Respectful) Education Act by state Sen. Mark Leno, D-San Francisco, adds lesbian, gay, bisexual and transgender people, as well as the disabled, into the existing list of underrepresented cultural and ethnic groups listed in the state's inclusionary education requirements.

"History should be honest," Brown said. "This bill revises existing laws that prohibit discrimination in education and en-sures that the important contributions of Americans from all backgrounds and walks of life are included in our history books."

Equality California Executive Director Roland Palencia called the new law "a monumental victory" for equality. "Thanks to the FAIR Education Act, California students, particularly LGBT youth, will find new hope and inspiration and experience a more welcoming learning environment."

Some conservatives opposed the bill and had urged Brown not to sign it.

"Jerry Brown has trampled the parental rights of the broad majority of California mothers and fathers who don't want their children to be sexually brainwashed," SaveCalifornia.com President Randy Thomasson said. "The only way parents can opt-out their kids from this immoral indoctrination is to opt them out of the entire public school system."

This is "the eighth school sexual indoctrination law forcing immorality on kids in California K-12 schools," he added, and "the broad majority of parents don't want their children be made to admire homosexuals, bisexuals and transsexuals."

The state Senate approved SB48 in April on a 23-14 vote; the Assembly passed it last week on a 50-26 vote.

The new law will enrich classroom lessons by better reflecting the state's diversity, Tom Torlakson, state superintendent of public instruction, said in a statement. "Our history is more complete when we recognize the contributions of people from all backgrounds and walks of life."

But due to budget cuts, the state won't create new K-8 curriculum materials until 2015.

The Blacks and Wetbacks are in the History Books, so why not Queers also. Plus the Muslims are trying to have their Laws and religion made law here in the U.S. by trying to do away with the "Laws Of The Land" put here and adopted by the White Man. BUT, what can you expect with the way out President and Congress has treated "Us Dumb American Citizens". "Dumb American Citizens" who continual votes those same Educated Idiots back into office at each election time.

NO HELP

Us Dumb Americans who owned our homes and cars live on a limited income and retired got nothing, each time S.S. gives us a raise the Insurance Companies take it. Why don't the Government give us a raise without the insurance companies taking it for once. $500.00 a Month would be fair. So why do Us Dumb Americans keep voting the same crooked congress people back into office? Cause we are Dumb and continue to vote for them.

WE DO NOT HAVE THE MONEY TO GIVE THEM IS WHY THEY
DO NOTHING FOR THE GENERAL PUBLIC.
BUT THEY SURE AS HELL WANT OUR VOTE

WHO DOES CONGRESSS LISTEN TO?

The people in congress do as they please and only listen and cater to the people and companies that give them money.

The bottom line is MONEY for Themselves.

I TOLD YOU SO

I told you so, See article below, It proves I was right about our Dumb Crooked Washington bunch. Us Dumb Americans vote and sent the same ones back to Washington and they cannot even speak for themselves, They have to have a Lobbyists speak and write their speeches and bills that they want to pass

Another promises by our President to get rid of lobbyists, but he did not say when he would.

How much did the Congress people get paid for letting the Lobbyists write their bills and speeches ?

CONGRESSIONAL RECORD

4A Sunday, Nov. 15

Lobbyists spoke for many lawmakers

The lobbyists drafted one statement for Democrats and another for Republicans, e-mail messages show.

By ROBERT PEAR
The New York Times

WASHINGTON — In the official record of the historic House debate on healthcare overhaul, the speeches of many lawmakers are brimming with similarities. Often, that was no accident.

Statements by more than a dozen lawmakers were ghostwritten, in whole or in part, by Washington lobbyists working for Genentech, one of the world's largest biotechnology companies.

E-mail messages obtained by *The New York Times* show that the lobbyists drafted one statement for Democrats, another for Republicans.

The lobbyists, employed by Genentech and by two Washington law firms, were remarkably successful in getting the statements printed in the Congressional Record under the names of different members of Congress.

Genentech, a subsidiary of the Swiss drug giant Roche, estimates that 42 House members picked up some of its talking points — 22 Republicans and 20 Democrats, an unusual bipartisan coup for lobbyists.

In an interview, Rep. Bill Pascrell Jr., D-N.J., said: "I regret that the language was the same. I did not know it was." He said he got his statement from his staff and "did not know where they got the information from."

Members of Congress submit statements for publication in the Congressional Record all the time, often with a decorous request to "revise and extend my remarks." It is unusual for so many revisions and extensions to match up word for word. It is even more unusual to find clear evidence that the statements originated with lobbyists.

The e-mail messages indicate that the statements were based on information supplied by Genentech employees to one of its lobbyists, Matthew L. Berzok, a lawyer at Ryan, MacKinnon, Vasapoli & Berzok who is identified as the "author" of the documents. The statements were disseminated by lobbyists at a big law firm, Sonnenschein Nath & Rosenthal.

In an e-mail message to fellow lobbyists on Nov. 5, two days before the House vote, Todd M. Weiss, senior managing director of Sonnenschein, said, "We are trying to secure as many House R's and D's to offer this/these statements for the record as humanly possible."

Weiss told the lobbyists to "conduct aggressive outreach to your contacts on the Hill to see if their bosses would offer the attached statements (or an edited version) for the record."

In separate statements using language suggested by the lobbyists, Rep. Blaine Luetkemeyer of Missouri and Wilson of South Carolina, both Republicans, said: "One of the reasons I have long supported the U.S. biotechnology industry is that it is a homegrown success story that has been an engine of creation in this country. Unfortunately many of the largest companies would seek to enter the biosimilar market have made their money by outsourcing their research to foreign countries like India."

In nearly identical words, three Republicans — Reps. K. Michael Conaway of Texas, Lynn Jenkins of Kansas and Terry of Nebraska — said they had criticized many provisions of the bill, "rightfully so."

But, each said, "I do believe the provisions relating to the creation of a market for biosimilar products is one area of the bill that strikes the appropriate balance in providing lower cost options."

On the House floor, Rep. Phil Hare of Ill., said his family had faced eviction when his father was sick. He said the House bill would save others from such hardship.

In a written addendum in the Congressional Record, Hare said the bill would also create high-paying jobs. His spokesman Timothy Schlittner said, "That part of his statement was drafted for us by Roche pharmaceutical company. It is something he agrees with."

38

ONLY ONE

Jim Wright from Texas listened and helped the people in his district and took phone calls himself.

Try and call your congressman and talk to him to day, HA Good Luck. Try to write to him and you may or may not receive an answer, Maybe in 3 months if at all,

Since the US Citizen now days is upset with Washington you might catch him at a Forum he may be holding since he is afraid he will lose the election You can talk to someone in his office if they are not on an 8 hour lunch break

U.S. GOVERNMENT NOSE

The U.S. tells other countries that we will give you money if you let us tell you how
to run your government
But,
When our Dumb Government gives a country money, the Dictator takes it for himself
Instead of helping the country

Most violations of tap water safety rules go unpunished

More than 20 percent of the U.S.' water treatment systems have broken federal laws, an analysis shows.

By CHARLES DUHIGG
The New York Times

More than 20 percent of the United States' water treatment systems have violated key provisions of the Safe Drinking Water Act over the last five years, according to a *New York Times* analysis of federal data.

That law requires communities to deliver safe tap water to local residents. But since 2004, the water provided to more than 49 million people has contained illegal concentrations of chemicals like arsenic or radioactive substances like uranium, as well as dangerous bacteria often found in sewage.

Regulators were informed of each of those violations as they occurred. But regulatory records show that fewer than 6 percent of the water systems that broke the law were ever fined or punished by state or federal officials, including those at the Environmental Protection Agency, which has ultimate responsibility for enforcing standards.

The problem, current and former government officials say, is that enforcing the Safe Drinking Water Act has not been a federal priority.

Studies indicate that drinking water contaminants are linked to millions of instances of illness within the United States each year.

Today, the Senate Environment and Public Works committee will question a high-ranking EPA official about the agency's enforcement of drinking-water safety laws. The EPA is expected to announce a new policy for how it polices the nation's 54,700 water systems.

"This administration has made it clear that clean water is a top priority," EPA spokeswoman Adora Andy said in response to questions regarding the agency's drinking water enforcement. EPA Administrator Lisa Jackson this year announced a wide-ranging overhaul of enforcement of the Clean Water Act, which regulates pollution into waterways.

An analysis of EPA data shows that Safe Drinking Water Act violations have occurred in parts of every state. In Ramsey, N.J., for instance, drinking water tests since 2004 have detected illegal concentrations of arsenic, a carcinogen, and the dry cleaning solvent tetrachloroethylene, which has also been linked to cancer. In New York state, 205 water systems have broken the law by delivering tap water that contained illegal amounts of bacteria since 2004.

This is another prime example as to what happens when the President and Congress does not take care of business here at home, Would not have happen if the U.S. would stop sticking our nose in other countries business

FRAGILE ALLIANCE

Pakistanis harass U.S. diplomats

HOW IN THE WORLD CAN THE U.S.A FIGHT A WAR WITH THIS HAPPENING?

The New York Times

ISLAMABAD — Parts of the Pakistani military and intelligence services are mounting what American officials describe as a campaign to harass U.S. diplomats, fraying relations at a crucial moment when the Obama administration is demanding more help to fight the Taliban and al Qaeda.

The campaign includes the refusal to extend or approve visas for more than 100 U.S. officials and the frequent searches of American diplomatic vehicles in major cities, said a U.S. official briefed on the cases.

The problems affected military attachés, CIA officers, development experts, junior-level diplomats and others, a senior American diplomat said. As a result, some American aid programs to Pakistan, which President Barack Obama has called a crucial ally, are "grinding to a halt," the diplomat said.

American helicopters used by Pakistan to fight militants can no longer be serviced because visas for 14 American mechanics have not been approved, the diplomat said.

Reimbursements to Pakistan of nearly $1 billion a year for its counterterrorism operations were suspended because embassy accountants had to leave the country.

Pakistani officials acknowledged the situation but said the menacing atmosphere results from American arrogance and provocations, like taking photographs in sensitive areas, and a lack of understanding of how divided Pakistanis are about the alliance with the United States.

The campaign comes after months of rising anti-American sentiment here.

ONE WORLD GOVERNMENT

In this One World Government suggested by some over seas, they would have the rich countries give their extra money to the poor nations until all countries were equal. This would do away with the stock market.

Boy, Are they behind the times, don't they know the U.S. is the World Government.

The U.S. fights a war when it want to.
The U.S. puts the military in charge of a country too keep the peace.
The U.S. gives money to Dictators when they want some.
The U.S. tells other governments how to run their business.
The U.S. puts World Crininals in jail with out Due Process Of The Law.
The U.S. tells countries who can and can not have the A-Bomb.
When two countries go to war the U.S. jumps right in and settles the matter.

So, Who is the World Government?

TAX

Our tax should be the same for all Personal and Business. It is not the fault of the rich that the worker is not educated or smart enough to make Big money. For the ones that receive their money from their rich father, Well they are the lucky ones.

Table 7
Federal Individual Income Tax Rates and Exemptions, 1913 - 1995

Years	Personal Exemptions			Rates (range in percent)	Taxable Income Brackets [a]	
	Single	Married-Joint Return	Dependents		Lowest: Amount Under	Highest: Amount Over
1913 - 15	$3,000	$4,000	None	1.0-7.0	20,000	$500,000
1916	3,000	4,000	None	2.0-15.0	20,000	2,000,000
1917	1,000	2,000	$200	2.0-67.0	2,000	2,000,000
1918	1,000	2,000	200	6.0-77.0	4,000	1,000,000
1919 - 20	1,000	2,000	200	4.0-73.0	4,000	1,000,000
1921	1,000	2,500 [a]	400	4.0-73.0	4,000	1,000,000
1922	1,000	2,500 [a]	400	4.0-56.0	4,000	200,000
1923	1,000	2,500 [a]	400	3.0-56.0	4,000	200,000
1924	1,000	2,500	400	1.5b-46.0	4,000	500,000
1925 - 28	1,500	3,500	400	1.125b-25.0	4,000	100,000
1929	1,500	3,500	400	0.375b-24.0	4,000	100,000
1930 - 31	1,500	3,500	400	1.125b-25.0	4,000	100,000
1932 - 33	1,000	2,500	400	4.0-63.0	4,000	1,000,000
1934 - 35	1,000	2,500	400	4.0c-63.0	4,000	1,000,000
1936 - 39	1,000	2,500	400	4.0c-79.0	4,000	5,000,000
1940	800	2,000	400	4.4c-81.1	4,000	5,000,000
1941	750	1,500	400	10.0c-81.0	2,000	5,000,000
1942 - 43 [d]	500	1,200	350	19.0c-88.0	2,000	200,000
1944 - 45	500	1,000	500	23.0-94.0 [e]	2,000	200,000
1946 - 47	500	1,000	500	19.0-86.45 [e]	2,000	200,000
1948 - 49 [f]	600	1,200	600	16.6-82.13 [e]	2,000	200,000
1950	600	1,200	600	17.4-84.36 [e]	2,000	200,000
1952 - 53	600	1,200	600	20.4-91.0 [e]	2,000	200,000
1954 - 63	600	1,200	600	20.0-91.0 [e]	2,000	200,000
1964	600	1,200	600	16.0-77.0	500	100,000
1965 - 67	600	1,200	600	14.0-70.0	500	100,000
1968	600	1,200	600	14.0-75.25 [g]	500	100,000
1969	600	1,200	600	14.0-77.0	500	100,000
1970	625	1,250	625	14.0-71.75	500	100,000
1971	675	1,350	675	14.0-70.0	500	100,000
1972 - 76	750	1,500	750	14.0-70.0	500	100,000
1977 - 78	750	1,500	750	0.-70.0	3,200	203,200
1979 - 81	1,000	2,000	1,000	0.0-70.0 [h]	3,400	215,400
1982	1,000	2,000	1,000	0.0-50.0	3,400	85,600
1983	1,000	2,000	1,000	0.0-50.0	3,400	109,400
1984	1,000	2,000	1,000	0.0-50.0	3,400 [i]	162,400 [i]
1985	1,040 [j]	2,080 [j]	1,040 [j]	0.0-50.0	3,540 [i]	169,020 [i]
1986	1,080 [i]	2,160 [i]	1,080 [i]	0.0-50.0	3,670 [i]	175,250 [i]
1987	1,900	3,800	1,900	11.0-38.5	3,000	90,000
1988	1,950 [k]	3,900 [k]	1,950 [k]	15.0-28.0	29,750	171,090
1989	2,000 [j,k]	4,000 [j,k]	2,000 [j,k]	15.0-28.0 [l]	30,950	149,250
1990	2,050 [j,k]	4,100 [j,k]	2,050 [j,k]	15.0-28.0 [l]	32,450	78,400
1991	2,150 [j,k]	4,300 [j,k]	2,150 [j,k]	15.0-31.0 [l]	34,000	82,150
1992	2,300 [j,k]	4,600 [j,k]	2,300 [j,k]	15.0-31.0	35,800	85,500
1993	2,350 [j,k]	4,700 [j,k]	2,350 [j,k]	15.0-39.6 [m]	36,900	250,000
1994	2,450 [j,k]	4,900 [j,k]	2,450 [j,k]	15.0-39.6 [m]	38,000	250,000
1995	2,500 [j,k]	5,000 [j,k]	2,500 [j,k]	15.0-39.6 [m]	39,000	256,500
1996	2,550	5,100	2,550	15 - 39.6	40,100	263,750
1997	2,650	5,300	2,650	15 - 39.6	41,200	271,050
1998	2,700	5,400	2,700	15 - 39.6	42,350	278,450
1999	2,750	5,500	2,750	15 - 39.6	43,050	283,150
2000	2,800	5,600	2,800	15-39.6	43,850	288,350

[a] Married filing joint return.

ACIR/Significant Features of Fiscal Federalism 2:

45

A luxury shopping center in downtown Beijing. China, the world's second-largest economy, spent tens of billions of dollars on the 2008 Olympics and has sent astronauts into space.
The Associated Press/Alexander F. Yuan

China still gets billions in aid

❯ Donor nations question the need to help an economic powerhouse.

By Gillian Wong
The Associated Press

BEIJING — China spent tens of billions of dollars on a dazzling 2008 Olympics. It has sent astronauts into space. It recently became the world's second-largest economy. Yet it gets more than $2.5 billion a year in foreign government aid — and taxpayers and lawmakers in donor countries are increasingly asking why.

With the global economic slowdown crimping government budgets, many countries are finding such generosity politically and economically untenable.

China says it's still a developing country in need of aid, while some critics say the money should go to poorer countries in Africa and elsewhere.

Germany and Britain have moved in recent months to reduce or phase out aid. Japan, long China's biggest donor, halted new low-interest loans in 2008.

"People in the U.K. or people in the West see the kind of flawless expenditure on the Olympics and the [Shanghai] Expo, and it's really difficult to get them to think the U.K. should still be giving aid to China," said Adrian Davis, head of the British government aid agency in Beijing.

Aid to China from individual donor countries averaged $2.6 billion a year in 2007-08, according to the latest figures from the Organization for Economic Cooperation and Development.

Ethiopia, where average incomes are 10 times as small, got $1.6 billion. Iraq got $9.462 billion and Afghanistan $3.475 billion.

Today's aid adds up to $1.2 billion a year from Japan, followed by Germany at about half that amount, then France and Britain.

The U.S. gave $65 million in 2008, mainly for targeted programs promoting safe nuclear energy, health, human rights and disaster relief.

Our taxes would be lower if the So So's in Washington would stop giving our money away, But, If they did there would be no kickback to our Great Leaders in Washington

"HOW TO GET CONGRESS ATTENTION"

If all Americans stop paying taxes for just two months it would cause Congress to set up and pay attention to the American Public who are burden down with so many different types of taxes, like City-State-Federal-Elect. Co's- and it would stop congress from giving money to Countries just to be able to tell them how to run their country, and if that did not get their attention go for another month.

They could not put all of us in jail, Plus, they would not be receiving a check. Hit them in the Pocket where it will really hurt them.

WHO RUNS THE PRESIDENTS OFFICE

Insurance Co.-Unions-Rich -Corporations

EYES OPENED

It finally took a Black President to wake us Dumb Americans up as to what all the trouble Congress and past Presidents have gotten us into,

Now how long will it take Us Dumb Americans to vote all of those Congress people out of office.

How long will Us Dumb Americans Make Phone Call, and Demonstrate to correct our Governments misdeeds?

WHY U.S. FACTORIES MOVED TO OTHER COUNTRIES

Just figured out why companies in the U.S. moved their factories to china and other countries.
POLLUTION AND MONEY
Smart move for ▓▓ us to let China and other deal with the Water and Air Pollution from our factories.

On the other hand people in the US are without jobs and in poverty.

WHO WINS?

SOLUTION:
Bring back to the US all company factories that do not pollute the US Water, Lakes and Air and send over to China our companies factories that pollute.

PROBLEM:
If all of our companies factories are in China and other countries and if the U.S. has to go to war, Where will we get factories and supplies to fight a war?

Jobless rate tops 10% for first time in 26 years; experts expect it to worsen

The rising unemployment rate could threaten the recovery if it saps consumer confidence.

By CHRISTOPHER S. RUGABER
The Associated Press

WASHINGTON — The unemployment rate has hit double digits for the first time since 1983 — and is likely to go higher.

The 10.2 percent jobless rate for October shows how weak the economy remains even though it is growing. The rising jobless rate could threaten the recovery if it saps consumers' confidence and makes them more cautious about spending as the holiday season approaches. Texas' jobless rate had edged up to 8.2 percent in September, the most recent available data for the state.

The October U.S. unemployment rate — reflecting nearly 16 million jobless people — jumped from 9.8 percent in September, the Labor Department said Friday. The job losses occurred across most industries, from manufacturing and construction to retail and financial.

Counting people who stopped looking for work or those who settled for part-time jobs, the jobless rate would be 17.5 percent. AP

Economists say the unemployment rate could surpass 10.5 percent next year because employers are reluctant to hire.

President Barack Obama called the new jobs report another illustration of why much more work is needed to spur business creation and consumer spending. Noting legislation he's signed

More on JOBLESS on 5C

DFWJoblog
Six unemployed North Texans share their experiences as they hunt for a job during difficult times at
star-telegram.com/business

It's official: Great Recession ended in June '09

❚ The news won't make much difference to the nearly 15 million in the U.S. without jobs.

By Jeannine Aversa
The Associated Press

WASHINGTON — The longest recession the country has endured since the Great Depression ended in June 2009, a group that dates the beginning and end of recessions said Monday.

The National Bureau of Economic Research, a panel of academic economists based in Cambridge, Mass., said the recession began in December 2007 and lasted 18 months. Previously, the longest post-World War II downturns were those in 1973-75 and in 1981-82. Both lasted 16 months.

The bureau decision makes official what many economists have believed for some time, that the recession ended in the summer of 2009. But it won't make much difference to most Americans, especially the nearly 15 million without jobs.

Americans are coping with 9.6 percent unemployment, scant wage gains, weak home values and the worst foreclosure market in decades.

President Barack Obama saw little reason to celebrate the group's finding.

Appearing at a town-hall meeting sponsored by CNBC, Obama said times are still very hard for people "who are struggling," including those who are out of work and many others who are having difficulty paying their bills.

"The hole was so deep that a lot of people out there are still hurting," the president said. It's going "to take more time to solve" an economic problem that was years in the making, he added.

The economy started growing again in the third quarter of 2009, after a record four straight quarters of declines. So the second quarter of 2009 marked the last quarter when the economy was shrinking. At that time, it contracted 0.7 percent, after suffering through much deeper declines. That factored into the bureau's decision to pinpoint the end of the recession in June.

Any downturn would mark the start of a new recession, not the continuation of the December 2007 recession, the bureau

Obama

said. That's important because if the economy starts shrinking again, it could mark the onset of a "double-dip" recession. For many economists, the last time that happened was in 1981-82.

To make its determination, the bureau looks at figures that make up the nation's gross domestic product, which measures the total value of goods and services produced within the United States. It also reviews incomes, employment and industrial activity.

The economy lost 7.3 million jobs in the 2007-09 recession, also the most in the post-World War II period.

The Great Depression lasted much longer. The United States suffered through a 43-month recession that ended in 1933. Then, it slid back into recession, which lasted for 13 months. That ended in

1938.

The bureau normally takes its time declaring that a recession has started or ended. For instance, it announced in December 2008 that the recession had started one year earlier.

Similarly, it declared in July 2003 that the 2001 recession was over; it ended 20 months earlier, in November 2001.

Its determination is of interest to economic historians — and political leaders. Recessions that occur on their watch pose political risks.

In President George W. Bush's eight years in office, the United States fell into two recessions. The first was March to November 2001. The second one started in December 2007.

Unemployment usually keeps rising well after a recession ends.

Unemployment spiked to 10.1 percent in October 2009, which was the highest in just over a quarter-century.

Some think that that figure could climb higher, perhaps hitting 10.3 percent by early next year. After the 2001 recession, for instance, unemployment didn't peak until June 2003 — 19 months later.

By the numbers
18 months The length of the recession, from December 2007 to June 2009

7.3 million Jobs lost during the recession

10.1 percent The unemployment rate in October 2009, the highest in just over a quarter-century

For BIG BUSINESS YES, Such as Banks, Elect & Gas Co's, & Insurance Co's, But not for the Consumer,

U.S. poverty rate expected to rise to 15% from 13.2%

▶ It would be the highest single-year increase since 1959.

By Hope Yen and Liz Sidoti
The Associated Press

WASHINGTON — The number of poor people in the U.S. is on track for a record increase on President Barack Obama's watch, with the ranks of the working-age poor approaching the 1960s levels that led to the national war on poverty.

Census figures for 2009 — the recession-ravaged first year of Obama's presidency — will be released Thursday, and demographers expect grim findings.

It's unfortunate timing for Obama and his party just seven weeks before elections and with control of Congress at stake.

The expected poverty rate increase — from 13.2 percent to about 15 percent — would be another blow to Democrats struggling to persuade voters to keep them in power.

"The most important anti-poverty effort is growing the economy and making sure there are enough jobs out there," Obama said Friday at a White House news conference.

He stressed his commitment to helping the poor rise into the middle class.

"If we can grow the economy faster and create more jobs, then everybody is swept up into that virtuous cycle."

Interviews with six demographers who closely track poverty trends found wide consensus that the 2009 figure will probably be 14.7 to 15 percent.

Should those estimates hold true, some 45 million people, or more than 1 in 7, were poor last year. It would be the highest single-year increase since the government began calculating poverty figures in 1959.

The previous high was in 1980, when the rate jumped 1.3 percentage points to 13 percent during the energy crisis.

Among the 18-64 working-age population, the demographers expect a rise beyond 12.4 percent from 11.7 percent.

That would make it the highest since at least 1965, when another Democratic president, Lyndon B. Johnson, launched the war on poverty, expanding the government's role in social welfare programs from education to healthcare.

"My guess is that politically these figures will be greeted with alarm and dismay, but they won't constitute a clarion call to action," said William Galston, a domestic policy aide for President Bill Clinton.

"I hope the parties don't blame each other for the desperate circumstances of desperate people. That would be wrong, in my opinion.

"But that's not to say it won't happen."

Lawrence Mead, a New York University political science professor, conservative and author of *The New Politics of Poverty: The Nonworking Poor in America*, said the figures will have a minimal impact in November.

"Poverty is not as big an issue right now as middle-class unemployment. That's a lot more salient politically right now," he said.

But if the report is as troubling as expected, Republicans in the midst of an increasingly strong

Poverty defined
The 2008 poverty level is $22,025 for a family of four, including only cash income before tax deductions. It excludes capital gains, accumulated wealth and noncash government aid such as tax credits or food stamps.

drive to win control of the House, if not the Senate, would get one more argument to make against Democrats in the home-stretch.

The GOP says voters should fire Democrats because Obama's economic fixes are hindering the economic recovery.

Rightly or wrongly, Republicans could cite a higher poverty rate as evidence.

Democrats are likely to counter that the economic woes — and the poverty increase — began under President George W. Bush with the near-collapse of the financial industry in late 2008.

Although that's true, it's far from certain that the Democratic explanation will sway voters who are already trending heavily toward the GOP in polls as worrisome economic news piles up.

Hispanics and blacks — traditionally solid Democratic constituencies — could be inclined to stay home in November if, as expected, the Census Bureau reports that many more of them were poor last year.

Beyond the fall, the findings could pressure Obama to expand government safety-net programs before his likely 2012 re-election bid even as Republicans criticize him about federal spending and annual deficits.

Those are areas of concern for independent voters, whose support is critical in elections.

All the U.S. has to do is bring back to the U.S. all American companies to bring the U,S, out of the Depression.

Legislators often violate law on using marijuana

Saturday 10-10-78

The claim by President Carter's departed drug adviser, Dr. Peter Bourne, that there are marijuana and cocaine users on the White House staff elicited indignant cries on Capitol Hill. Sen. Howard Baker, R - Tenn., demanded an investigation. Speaker Tip O'Neill threatened any pot users in his office with instant dismissal.

They might well sniff a little further in the halls of Congress. An intimate study discloses that at least 26 House members and five senators are marijuana smokers, most of them on a regular basis.

The survey by investigators Ken Cummins and Lois Romano does not identify any of the violators. On grounds that members of Congress should obey the laws they enact, we have conducted our own investigation to learn their identities.

WE HAVE PICKED up a few names, but we have gathered enough evidence to mention only one. He is the powerful and popular Rep. John Burton, D - Calif., a mod congressman with longish hair, a sporty mustache and a liberal voting record. He is a chain smoker who habitually douses his cigarettes in an empty soda can during congressional proceedings.

Sources familiar with what goes on in the backrooms told us that Burton is "probably one of the biggest users of marijuana in the House." He has also been identified as a cocaine devotee by Gino DelPrete, a man - about - San Francisco and convicted heroin trafficker who started the topless dancing craze in the early '60s.

Jack Anderson

In sworn testimony, an undercover narcotics agent has alleged that he was approached by DelPrete who wanted to procure some cocaine. The dapper DelPrete said he wanted the illegal drug for a powerful friend, a political figure who could pull strings. DelPrete identified the friend, testified the agent, as Congressman Burton.

IN HIS UNDERCOVER role as a narcotics pusher, the agent said he slipped DelPrete a quarter - ounce of a legal substitute that looked like the real thing. Other sources have confirmed the incident.

Retorted the accused congressman: "I grew up with Gino in San Francisco, but I don't know what the hell he's talking about." Burton said he had never asked DelPrete for drugs and couldn't imagine why he would say such a thing.

Cummins and Romano have summarized their Capitol Hill findings in an article which will be published in the November issue of Playboy magazine. The manuscript will say:

"Of the 435 House members, 101 answered the poll, and 26 of them admitted to having smoked grass. In the Senate, only 17 of the 100 members answered the survey, and not one confessed to smoking dope. However, subsequent interviews identified five dedicated Senate pot smokers."

OTHER SOURCES estimate that between 10 percent and 20 percent of the 535 members of Congress have sampled at least pot. Surprisingly, the manuscript reports that most of the admitted marijuana smokers in the House are between the ages of 35 and 60, rather than the younger generation of congressmen in the 25 - 35 age bracket.

"In fact," they report, "according to survey reponses, there are two regular pot smokers in the House between 60 and 75."

It's no secret, of course, that millions of Americans smoke pot. The widespread use of marijuana by congressmen, therefore, might seem innocuous. But young men and women are languishing in prison for doing no less.

In West Plains, Mo., for example, Jerry Mitchell, the 21 - year - old son of blind parents, was sentenced in 1976 to 12 years in prison for selling $5 worth of pot to an undercover cop. The sentence was later reduced to seven years.

In nearby Jefferson City, 20 - year - old Evelyn Wilson is serving a five - year sentence for purchasing an ounce of pot and "selling" half of it to the young man she was dating. He turned out to be a narcotics agent, who was allegedly dating her to learn about the local drug culture.

After reading the above, Is there any question
In your mind now as to what goes on in
Washington and how the U. S, President and
Congress has gotten this country into such a mess
We now live with.

"WHAT IS GOOD FOR CONGRESS IS NOT
GOOD FOR THE AMERICAN CITIZEN'

Insider Trading OK Inside Congress

Astonishingly, congressmen and their aides are legally permitted to trade stocks on deep-inside information. Many are doing it and profiting handsomely. If those on Wall Street did this, they'd go to jail.

By Jim Meyers

AN INVESTOR IS PRIVY TO INFORMATION that Congress will pass legislation providing an investment tax credit for companies in the solar energy business. Based on that information, he buys shares in a firm producing solar panels, then watches the stock rise after the news breaks, sells the shares, and makes a quick profit.

If this happened within a corporation, it would be illegal insider trading. But if the investor is a member of Congress, it's all fair game; the insider trading laws passed by the House and Senate do not apply to the very legislators who passed them.

Turns out there's nothing in the current laws that prevents members of Congress, or their aides, from insider trading, or even from providing someone else, say, a major campaign contributor, with inside information, according to Bloomberg.

"A 2004 study of the results of stock trading by United States senators during the 1990s found that senators on average beat the market by 12 percent a year," writes Stephen M. Bainbridge of UCLA law school. "In sharp contrast, U.S. households on average underperformed the mar-

ket by 1.4 percent a year and even corporate insiders on average beat the market by only about 6 percent a year during that period.

"A reasonable inference is that some senators had access to — and were using — nonpublic information about the companies in whose stock they trade."

The Wall Street Journal discloses that in 2008 and 2009, at least 72 congressional aides traded shares of companies that their bosses helped oversee. The aides' employers include Senate Majority Leader Harry Reid and House Speaker Nancy Pelosi.

Many of the aides' trades involved companies in industries dependent

> **+12%** Senator
>
> On average, the amount by which a U.S. senator **beat** the market versus the amount by which a U.S. household **underperformed** the market.
>
> **-1.4%**

on government help, such as financial services and renewable energy, the *Journal* analysis found.

Congressional staffers, not to mention legislators, routinely attend high-level, closed-door briefings or engage in conversations that provide access to nonpublic information, which can have a bearing on whether to buy or sell stocks.

The aides identified by the *Journal* said they didn't profit from trades based on any information "gathered in the halls of Congress. Even if they had done so, it would be legal, because insider-trading laws don't apply to Congress."

Rules dating back to the 1960s do require all members of Congress and nearly 3,000 of the highest-paid aides to disclose financial information, including capital gains from trading securities, but they need to file only once a year. And the disclo-

next page

55

TAKING STOCK A new act would prohibit members of Congress (assembled here in a hearing room) from taking part in dubious trades.

sure requires only ranges of dollar amounts, not specific figures.

When Nancy Pelosi became House speaker in 2006, she pledged to "drain the swamp" of congressional misdeeds and oversee the "most ethical and honest Congress in history." But a member of her own staff is included among the congressional aides cited in the *Journal* report.

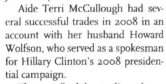

Rep. Slaughter, Rep. Baird

Aide Terri McCullough had several successful trades in 2008 in an account with her husband Howard Wolfson, who served as a spokesman for Hillary Clinton's 2008 presidential campaign.

They profited by trading shares of Freddie Mac and Fannie Mae a mere two days before the govern-ment authorized emergency funding for the two companies.

Shares of their stock rose about 40 percent on the day Wolfson bought and sold the shares. For his part, Wolfson insists that he made the trades without telling his wife or getting any information from her.

Joel Brubaker, chief of staff for Rep. Shelley Moore Capito, R-W.Va., a member of the House Financial Services Committee, made money trading in financial services firms last year, according to filings.

Karen Brown, an aide to Sen. Mike Crapo, R-Idaho, a member of the Senate Banking Committee, traded Bank of America stock seven times in 2009.

Chris Miller, Nevada Democrat Harry Reid's top energy policy adviser, nearly doubled an investment in a renewable-energy company in 2008.

In an effort to rein in questionable trading, Rep. Brian Baird, D-Wash., and Louise Slaughter, D-N.Y., have proposed the Stop Trading on Congressional Knowledge (STOCK) Act. It would prohibit congressional insiders from trading in financial markets based on nonpublic information they learn on the job, and require them to make their financial transactions public within 90 days of a purchase or sale. But the bill has languished since 2006.

"Congressional staff are often privy to information, and an unscrupulous person could profit off that knowledge," said Vincent Morris, a spokesman for Rep. Slaughter. "The public should be outraged there is no law specifically banning this." □

What is good for Congress is not good for the American Citizen.

SHOW ME THE DOOR, THEN SHOW ME THE MONEY

▶ ACCORDING TO THE **NATIONAL TAXPAYERS UNION**, there are 16 former members of Congress convicted of serious crimes who remain eligible for pensions with a combined value just shy of $1 million per year. They are:

Politician	Party & State	Crime(s)	Year Convicted	Pension in 2011
Rep. John Murphy	D-N.Y.	Conspiracy, accepting unlawful gratuity, Abscam scandal	1980	$88,688
Rep. Frederick Richmond	D-N.Y.	Tax evasion, drug possession	1982	$33,131
Rep. Mario Biaggi	D-N.Y.	Bribery/Wedtech scandal	1988	$67,277
Rep. Albert Bustamante	D-Texas	Racketeering, accepting bribes	1993	$18,803
Sen. David Durenberger	R-Minn.	Misuse of Senate funds	1995	$96,575
Rep. Larry Smith	D-Fla.	Tax evasion, false campaign filing	1995	$33,738
Rep. Carl C. Perkins	D-Ky.	Bank fraud, false campaign filing	1994	$14,500*
Rep. Carroll Hubbard	D-Ky.	Campaign finance violations, theft of U.S. property, obstructing justice	1994	$72,964
Rep. Walter Fauntroy	D-D.C.	False financial disclosure	1995	$62,192
Rep. Joseph Kolter	D-Pa.	Conspiracy/congressional post office scandal	1996	$53,449
Rep. Mary Rose Oakar	D-Ohio	Campaign finance violations	1997	$61,432
Rep. Austin J. Murphy	D-Pa.	Voter fraud	1999	$87,832
Rep. James Traficant	D-Ohio	Ten corruption charges	2002	$44,992
Gov. John Rowland	R-Conn.	"Honest services fraud" as governor of Conn. (served in Congress 1985-91)	2004	$8,400**
Rep. Randall Cunningham	R-Calif.	Conspiracy to commit bribery and fraud, tax evasion	2005	$71,519
Rep. Bob Ney	R-Ohio	Conspiracy to commit bribery and other offenses, making false statements	2006	$20,062

*approximate; will qualify in 2016 | **approximate; will qualify in 2019

Dimming freedom

I grew up in the depression era. We used kerosene lamps with wicks that you trimmed, otherwise they smoked; then they made Coleman lanterns with butane fuel that had the fragile little sacks that you had to be careful with, but they did put out more light.

What a relief when they came out with the light bulb — although our farm northwest of Grapevine had no electricity because neither the Rural Electric Administration nor the Texas Power and Light Co. would run their poles to our house because we lived halfway between the two lines. It was only when Lake Grapevine was built and it cut off the lines for REA that TP&L ran electricity through our property; then Mother and Daddy were able to get electricity. That was 1951.

I have been buying up 60-, 75- and 100-watt bulbs because those funky looking light bulbs the government is trying to force us to use do not give off enough light. We might as well buy a kerosene lamp and start over to the 1930s.

We have become a country in which Congress can dictate to the public what we can use.

— Marie Stearns, Bedford

Your Congressman Joe Barton and a few others wants to tell the Colleges who should play in the Championship game so, Why not tell us Americans what Light Bulbs we can Use, Would not have happen if US DUMB AMERICANS would stop voting these Idiots back into office. Can anyone not see what those Idiots in Washington have done and are trying to do to America and the American People? If they get their way our homes will belong to the Federal Government and we would get a small allowance to use as they would also tell you how you could spend that money.

Americans see politics paralyzing government

By STEVEN THOMMA
McClatchy Newspapers

WASHINGTON — An overwhelming majority of Americans think that the federal government is gridlocked by partisan fighting and turf battles and can't accomplish anything, according to a new McClatchy-Ipsos poll.

Yet the anger and frustration with Washington aren't directed solely at either party and don't automatically add up to a tidal wave against the governing Democrats in this year's elections for control of Congress, the poll suggested.

In fact, Americans tilt slightly against Republicans as to which party they blame more. They also give a 10-point edge to Democrats when they're asked which party they'd vote for if the congressional elections were today.

"Overall, the poll suggests a level of disgust with politics as usual," said Clifford Young, a senior vice president with Ipsos Public Affairs, which conducted the survey. "Americans are basically angry at incumbents and Washington. This isn't necessarily directed at any one party."

Four in 5 Americans said Washington can't accomplish anything because of fighting between the political parties and branches of the government, the poll found. Only 17 percent disagreed.

The sentiment is deeply held: Fifty-one percent strongly agree that gridlock renders the government impotent. It's also felt across the political spectrum, with 81 percent of Republicans, 80 percent of Democrats and 79 percent of independents agreeing that the government is bogged down.

Underscoring the public disgust: The ranks of people who think the country is on the right track hit the lowest level since President Barack Obama took office last year: only 34 percent. Almost twice as many, 60 percent, said it is on the wrong track.

The country's mood improved at first under Obama, with those saying the country was headed in the right direction rising from 42 percent shortly after he took office to a high of 55 percent in early May. It's dropped ever since, rooted in anxiety about the recession and unemployment.

MARCH 3, 2010

March 3, 2010 is here and the election is over and most all incumbents are re-elected by US DUMB AMERICANS again after complaining for the past two years on how the U.S. Government is run by Idiots.

Spending bill goes through after senator lifts objection

Jim Bunning criticizes Democrats for flouting the "pay-go" terms.

By HALIMAH ABDULLAH and DAVID LIGHTMAN
McClatchy Newspapers

WASHINGTON — By a vote of 78-19, the Senate passed funding Tuesday night to revive government programs that aid jobless people, highway projects and other initiatives that had shut down for nearly 48 hours because of Sen. Jim Bunning's increasingly unpopular one-man stand against the measure.

The deadlock ended Tuesday when the Kentucky Republican relented to growing pressure not only from angry constituents but also from Senate colleagues from both parties.

The House of Representatives passed the measure last week. Once President Barack Obama signs the measure, $10 billion can be spent to keep most of the programs operating for about a month.

Bunning wanted the provisions paid for, but other senators said these were emergency measures and didn't need to be offset.

The pressure on Bunning steadily grew. On Tuesday, the Senate spent most of the day debating the measure — with most senators, including some from his own party, pleading for him to drop his objection.

On Tuesday evening, he did.

"I hope Senate Democrats tonight vote for their own pay-fors and show Americans that they are committed to fiscal discipline," Bunning said.

"I will be watching them closely and checking off the hypocrites one by one."

THE ASSOCIATED PRESS/HARRY HAMBURG
Sen. Jim Bunning had said he wanted the $10 billion measure offset by spending cuts elsewhere.

Bunning stressed that he supports the programs and criticized Senate Majority Leader Harry Reid, D-Nev., and other Democrats for not sticking to recently passed "pay-go" provisions, which require paying for many new programs with readily available funds rather than with additional borrowing.

One of Tuesday night's procedural votes focused on Bunning's amendment to offset the $10 billion price tag of the Democratic-backed 30-day extension of funding for jobless benefits and other government initiatives. That effort failed.

This week, two additional votes will be held on his proposals to offset the costs of a longer-term benefits bill.

While trying to blame Democrats for mishandling the entire matter, some Republicans have also distanced themselves from Bunning.

"This is one senator," said Sen. John Cornyn of Texas, a chief political strategist for Senate Republicans. "This does not represent the position of the caucus."

This report includes material from *The New York Times.*

'NO GUTS--NO GLORY FOR REP. NO BACKBONE BUNNING'

Course all those other Senators that put pressure on No Backbone Bunning are afraid of losing their next election if Bunning stuck to his position.

GOP fundraising pitch appeals to fear

The Associated Press

WASHINGTON — Barack Obama is "The Joker." Nancy Pelosi is portrayed as Cruella De Vil, and Harry Reid as Scooby-Doo — all part of a Republican Party pitch to fundraisers.

Tucked into the 72-page PowerPoint presentation to GOP fundraisers in Boca Raton, Fla., last month was a direct call to exploit "extreme negative feelings" toward Democrats using tactics that even Republican leaders said were out of line.

"What can you sell when you do not have the White House, the House or the Senate . . . ?" one slide asks.

"Save the country from tending toward Socialism!" it replies.

Political groups and parties often use highly charged language to motivate their base of voters and contributors. But the GOP document is unusual in revealing a strategy in such candid detail.

Republicans tried Thursday to dissociate themselves from the imagery and language of the presentation, which was first reported by the Politico news Web site.

Republican National Committee Chairman Michael Steele called the images inappropriate.

"Clearly it's not something that I would tolerate and certainly would not want presented to me, and we're dealing with it administratively," said Steele, who said he learned of the document Wednesday. "This is the line that we won't tolerate nor cross in the RNC."

The Democratic National Committee condemned the document as "Republican fear mongering" using "the most despicable kind of imagery, tactics and rhetoric imaginable." Democratic spokesman Brad Woodhouse said the presentation encourages fundraisers to exploit "extreme negative feelings toward the existing administration."

The above article shows why the American Public has lost all respect for Congress

But, US DUMB AMERICANS will vote

those Republicans and Democrats

back into office again come the next

election.

This is what is wrong with America, "US DUMB AMERICAN'S" vote in a bunch of dumb congress people who pick dummies for the Supreme Court who knows nothing about filling out his/her own tax returns. A Supreme Court Justice who cannot follow or understand the filing instructions or, he was trying to cheat the U. S. Government, which I think. How in the world can this man be a Supreme Court Justice and decide cases that come up before him concerning the U.S. Tax laws when he does not know the law and cannot understand the IRS instructions?

No were but in America could this happen.

Obama now using strategy he decried

As a presidential candidate, he said he was opposed to "50-plus-one."

By CALVIN WOODWARD
The Associated Press

WASHINGTON — President Barack Obama is trying to achieve a healthcare overhaul the way he once said it couldn't, and shouldn't, be done.

He wants congressional Democrats to move ahead without Republican support and pass the legislation with a bare majority in the Senate instead of the broader majority he favored as a candidate.

Obama has tried to get Republicans behind him. Having failed, he's reverting to a "50-plus-one" strategy that he called a losing proposition when he was a candidate for the Democratic presidential nomination.

Republican Rep. Eric Cantor of Virginia complained Thursday that Obama had "done a 180" by resorting to the fast-track procedure, given his past views as a candidate.

White House press secretary Robert Gibbs denied that, insisting that Obama was "talking about electoral strategy, not vote-counting in the House and the Senate," in his October 2007 remarks. In fact, Obama was talking about both, and more.

AP/CHARLES DHARAPAK
White House Press Secretary Robert Gibbs

Cantor made his remarks on the House floor, where he also defended his party's use of special parliamentary tactics to enact laws with a simple majority. He was wrong in stating that Republicans had mostly used the tactics to pass bipartisan legislation.

A look at how the claims stack up to the facts:

The claim: Gibbs at first said Obama was talking only about how to get elected when he criticized the 50-plus-one strategy in an October 2007 interview with the *Concord Monitor* in New Hampshire. Pressed, Gibbs then said Obama meant "you're not going to get legislation through Congress if only 50 percent plus one in the country think it's a good idea."

The facts: Obama wasn't talking about polls or public opinion — or only about electoral politics — in the interview.
"You've got to break out of what I call the . . . 50-plus-one pattern of presidential politics, which is you have nasty primaries where everybody's disheartened, then you divide the country 45 percent on one side 45 percent on the other and 10 percent in the middle," he began. "Battle it out and then maybe you eke out a victory of 50 plus one, and then you can't govern."

The claim: House Majority Leader Steny Hoyer, D-Md., argued that Republicans had used the same fast-track process to enact major legislation along partisan lines when they were in charge of Congress. Cantor denied it.

The facts: Of the 10 occasions from 1995 to 2005 when Republicans were in the Senate majority and used reconciliation to pass bills, seven passed with deep partisan divisions. In 2005, for example, Republicans used reconciliation to muscle through a deficit reduction bill that restricted Medicaid payments. It passed with 50 Republicans in favor, all Democrats against and Vice President Dick Cheney voting to break a tie.

Sen. Olympia Snowe of Maine was the only Republican to support a one-time bonus payment last fall for seniors on Social Security. Twelve Democrats opposed the measure.

Social Security recipients won't get raise again

Retirement ❯ The cost-of-living adjustment is based on inflation.

By Stephen Ohlemacher
The Associated Press

WASHINGTON — The government is expected to announce this week that Social Security recipients will go another year without an increase in monthly benefits.

It would be only the second year without an increase since automatic adjustments for inflation were adopted, in 1975. The first was this year.

Cost-of-living adjustments are automatically set each year by an inflation measure that was adopted by Congress in the 1970s. Based on inflation this year, the trustees who oversee Social Security project no COLA for 2011.

The projection will be made official Friday, when the Bureau of Labor Statistics releases inflation estimates for September.

The timing couldn't be worse for Democrats as they approach an election in which they are in danger of losing their House majority and possibly their Senate majority as well.

"If you're the ruling party, this is not the sort of thing you want to have happening two weeks before an election," said Andrew Biggs, a resident scholar at the American Enterprise Institute.

Democrats have been working hard to make Social Security an election-year issue, running political ads and holding news conferences to accuse Republicans of plotting to privatize the national retirement program.

Social Security was the primary source of income for 64 percent of retirees who got benefits in 2008, according to the Social Security Administration. A third relied on Social Security for at least 90 percent of their income.

A little more than 58.7 million people receive Social Security or Supplemental Security Income.

The average Social Security benefit is about $1,072 a month.

Social Security recipients got a one-time bonus of $250 in spring 2009 as part of the government's massive economic recovery package. President Barack Obama lobbied for another one

Social Security
The Social Security Administration is expected to announce Friday that retirees and disabled Americans will see no increase in benefits for 2011 for the second straight year, based on a formula tied to inflation. Here's a look at who gets benefits:
- Total beneficiaries: 58.7 million
- Social Security recipients: 53.5 million
- Supplemental Security Income recipients: 7.9 million
- Recipients of Social Security and SSI: 2.7 million
- Average monthly Social Security payment: $1,072
- Average monthly SSI payment: $499
- Social Security is the primary source of income for 64 percent of recipients.
- One-third of recipients rely on Social Security for at least 90 percent of their income.
- Early retirement age: 62
- Full retirement age: 66, rising to 67 for people born after 1959
Source: Social Security Administration

last fall when it became clear that seniors wouldn't get an increase in monthly benefit payments in 2010.

Congress took up the issue, but a proposal by Sen. Bernie Sanders, I-Vt., died when 12 Democrats and independent Sen. Joe Lieberman of Connecticut joined Senate Republicans to block it. Sen. Olympia Snowe of Maine was the only Republican to support the measure.

Federal law requires the Social Security Administration to base annual payment increases on the Consumer Price Index for Urban Wage Earners and Clerical Workers, which measures inflation.

Officials compare inflation in the third quarter of each year with the third quarter of the previous year.

Sanders said he expects older voters to be angry when they learn that there will be no increase again.

Since Obama could not get his campain money from all the People on S.S. he let the Insurance Co's raise our S.S. Insurance that is than given to Him.
"SEE NEXT PAGE"

House to eye Social Security payout

The Associated Press

WASHINGTON — The House will vote in November on providing $250 payments to Social Security recipients to make up for the lack of a cost-of-living increase for next year, House Speaker Nancy Pelosi said Thursday.

The Social Security Administration is expected to announce today that more than 58 million retirees and disabled Americans will go a second year without an increase in benefits.

Pelosi said she will schedule a vote on a bill to provide the $250 payments when Congress returns for a lame-duck session after the Nov. 2 congressional elections. The payments would be similar to those provided by the government's massive economic recovery package last year.

But even if Pelosi can get the House to approve a second payment, the proposal faces opposition in the Senate.

"All members of Congress should join us in supporting this legislation which will be fiscally responsible and upholds our bedrock promise of economic security for our na-tion's seniors," Pelosi said in a statement.

Cost-of-living adjustments, or COLAs, are set automatically each year by an inflation measure that was adopted by Congress in the 1970s. Because consumer prices are lower than two years ago, the last time a COLA was awarded, the trustees who oversee Social Security project that there will be no benefit increase for 2011.

The projection will be made official today, when the Bureau of Labor Statistics releases inflation estimates for September.

Washington is again pulling the WOOL over the eyes of Us Dumb Americans. Does Americans not know that this increase and the one we got last year will not be add in our check once the depression is over?

Once the depression is over and we receive our regular cost of living that will stay with us for the rest of our lives, The money we received last year and this year if we get one was for one time only. BUT, US DUMB AMERICANS WILL VOTE THAT WASHINGTON BUNCH BACK INTO OFFICE ONCE AGAIN.

"SEE TWO EXAMPLES BELOW"

How our great leaders in WASHINGTON are turning more AMERICAN CITIZEN into Poverty with their Idiot Laws, Why? Because Us Dumb Americans keep voting the Old Ones back into office.

Why does a retired American that receives a Social Security Check and a small Railroad Retirement check have the Amount of the Railroad check deducted From their S.S. check? He worked and earned each.

Legislation aims to end widows' tax

By Kimberly Hefling
The Associated Press

WASHINGTON — Tens of thousands of the nation's war widows find it perplexing and downright disrespectful to their late military husbands: To fully collect on insurance their husbands bought for them, they must marry another man.

In addition, the widows must remarry when they are 57 or older. Those who remarry earlier miss out, as do widows who never remarry.

At the heart of the issue is a policy known as the "widows' tax."

It says a military spouse whose loved one dies from a service-related cause can't collect both survivor's benefits and the full annuity benefits from insurance the couple bought from the Defense Department at retirement. Instead, the amount of the annuity payment is reduced by the amount of the monthly survivor benefit.

Time after time, members of Congress have promised to help the 55,000 affected widows, but laws enacted to help them have only created a more complicated system.

So what's remarriage got to do with it? Very little, as it turns out. The marriage condition was stuck into the law by Congress as it tried to help the survivors retain certain benefits if they remarried late in life, as is the case with other federal annuities. Because Congress hasn't been able to come up with the money to help all the widows, relief has been limited to that group. The result is an all but incomprehensible mess.

"I've never even wanted to date, much less remarry," said Nichole Haycock, a mother of three teenagers in Lawton, Okla., whose 38-year-old military husband died in 2002. "I already married the love of my life. Why would you bring that as a factor?"

Sen. Bill Nelson, D-Fla., and 10 other senators filed legislation last week to help the widows.

"This has always been an issue of the military doing the right thing and living up to its promises," Nelson said in a statement.

66

12A Monday, March 28, 2011

Rising Medicare premiums may wipe out Social Security boost

The government is projecting a slight cost-of-living increase in benefits for Social Security recipients next year, but for most recipients the increase will be eaten up by rising Medicare premiums. Recipients shouldn't receive any less than they got last year, however — regulations prohibit premium increases from cutting benefits below last year's levels. **12A**

Social Security payments, Medicare premiums to rise

One may wipe out the other, resulting in no real increase for millions.

By Stephen Ohlemacher
The Associated Press

WASHINGTON — Millions of retired and disabled people in the United States had better brace for another year with no increase in Social Security payments.

The government is projecting a slight cost-of-living adjustment for Social Security benefits next year, the first increase since 2009. But for most beneficiaries, rising Medicare premiums threaten to wipe out any increase in payments, leaving them without a raise for a third straight year.

About 45 million people — 1 in 7 — receive both Medicare and Social Security. By law, beneficiaries have their Medicare Part B premiums, which cover doctor visits, deducted from their Social Security payments each month.

When Medicare premiums rise more than Social Security payments, millions of people living on fixed incomes don't get raises. On the other hand, most don't get pay cuts, either, because a provision prevents higher Part B premiums from reducing Social Security payments for most people.

Medicare premiums are absorbing a growing share of Social Security benefits, according to a report by the Congressional Research Service.

Social Security recipients spend, on average, 9 percent of their benefits on Medicare Part B premiums plus 3 percent on premiums for the Medicare prescription drug program.

By 2078, people just retiring would spend nearly one-third of their benefits on premiums for both Medicare programs, the report said. Also, when premiums for the prescription drug program increase, as they do almost every year, they can result in a pay cut for Social Security recipients.

By law, Social Security cost-of-living adjustments are determined each year by a government measure of inflation. When consumer prices go up, so do payments. When consumer prices fall, payments stay flat until prices rebound.

My S.S check has gone up, but the Insurance got all the raises for the past 15 years.

HOW MUCH MONEY DOES OR DID THE PRESIDENT GET FROM THE INSURANCE COMPANIES? A BUNCH.

The Government is not going to let you keep any or very little Of the money we worked for.

A federal fairy tale

Now let me get this straight. I will not, for the second year, get an increase in my Social Security, not even enough to cover the raise last year in Medicare premiums, which decreased my already low retirement income. Yet my expenses are on the rise and the government is telling me the "recession" is over, go spend some money, enjoy life and all is well. Could someone read me another fairy tale?

I will certainly be watching, along with all the other Social Security recipients, to see if members of Congress give themselves a raise in January

— Cecelia Gilbreath, Fort Worth

Too ideological

Absolutely incredible! Both U.S. senators from Texas, John Cornyn and Kay Bailey Hutchison, last week voted against a bill giving tax breaks to U.S. multinational corporations as an incentive for bringing jobs back to the United States — at a time when we need to be creating more middle-class jobs.

How do these folks keep getting elected? Have we become so ideological that we ignore good bills just because they come from the other party?

— Dave Robinson, Fort Worth

Thank Heaven Kay Bailey Hutchison did not win the Governors race against Rick Perry.

The above article above shows what is wrong in Washington., Cornyn and Hutchison both are part of the cause of our USA Citizens out of jobs and they have no intention of helping the USA get out of this depression.

Come on Tea Party, Liberals and New Candates, run like yours and my life depends on you winning the election. The Dallas Texas area of voters and Texas should be ashamed for keeping these two in office

I am 80 years of age and my wife and I are retired and do not have to depend on a job, But if the insurance companies keep taking money from our S.S. check each year with out a raise and once they get the whole check I guess we are than suppose to die. A 10% increase of our insurance is predicted this next year and I'am sure we will not receive a 10% increase in our S.S. check or retirement check Guess how much money Obama got from the Insurance Companies.

Come on TEXANS wake up to what Washington is doing to us,

Reno blocks Palestinian's release to review papers

BRADENTON, Fla. — Attorney General Janet Reno blocked the release of a Palestinian man jailed for three years without charges, federal officials said Tuesday.

The government maintains that Mazen Al-Najjar, 43, had links to Mideast terrorists and was a threat to national security. Al-Najjar denied the allegations. Not even his lawyers have ever seen the evidence against him.

Reno blocked Al-Najjar's release until 5 p.m. Friday, saying in an order given to lawyers in the case that she wanted to "personally review the appropriateness" of allowing his immediate release.

The article above is a prime example of the U.S. Government Lawyers doing the same thing that other countries do. The U.S. Government and news people tell the U.S. Citizens about how bad the governments of other countries are by putting people in jail for a long time without a trial or ever bring charges aganist them. This is a prime example of the Pot calling the Kettle Black. Prime example of U.S. Lawyers, and the Attorney General.

I remember when the US Newspapers and government made fun and degraded Russia and showing a picture of women in Russia working outside cleaning streets and digging out broken water lines, now the american women are doing the same. Maybe in Russia they had "Equal Rights for Women" before the U.S. did.

69

QUESTIONS

MISTAKES THAT THE U.S.A. CANNOT AFFORD

"A-Bomb That Moved Across The U.S. Undetected"

1. Who had authority over the storage of the A-Bomb?
2. Who had authority to take the A-Bomb out of storage and who gave him authority?
3. Who had the authority to put the A-Bomb on the Air Force plane?
4. Where was the Bomb headed to?
5. Who had the authority to take the Bomb off the plane?
6. Was there shipping papers with this Bomb and who signed the papers?
7. Who was to receive this Bomb after it was taken off the plane?
8. Who discovered the Bomb?
9. How could the Pilot and Crew not know they had the Bomb on board?

A-Bomb Fuses Shipped To A Foreign Country

1. Who requested the fuses?
2. Who in the company authorized the shipment to a foreign country?
3. Who arranged the shipment to another country?
4. Who was in charge of storing the fused?
5. Who had authority to take fuses out of storage and who requested that he do so?

With mistakes like the above, Iran should have no trouble getting hold of plans and equipment and fuses to build the Bomb.

Maybe it was not a mistake and was carried out by Terrorist, Terrorist within our Government ranks which the US has allowed to operate in the military and private sector.. Was there any Muslims involved in either one of the above?

Serving his country, preserving his faith

Army Capt. Tejdeep Singh Rattan, in turban, stands with other graduates during an Army officer basic training graduation ceremony at Fort S Houston in San Antonio on Monday. Rattan is the first Sikh to complete the course since 1984 without having to give up the unshorn hair manda by his faith. He had received an exemption from the Army's uniform policy that effectively bars Sikhs from enlisting. Only a handful of s individual religious exemptions are ever granted. "I'm feeling very humbled. I'm a soldier," he said. "This has been my dream."

Capt. Rattan must be a High Ranking Spy for the military since being to rise to the rank of Capt.. If he goes on and rises to the rank to be included in the Joint Chief of Staffs will he change the uniform for all military people to wear the Ushorn head piece and a Beard?

I remember when I was in the military I caught HELL if my hat did not conform to the rules on how I should wear the hat. Plus, not being clean shaven no matter what my faith was. Plus, I was not given Liberty to go ashore. Course those Joint Chief of Staff members are a bunch of Ass Kissers, they are letting the Muslims tell them how to run the military and what the Dress Code should be.

Obama's Islam Tact

While cultivating peaceful relationships with Muslims is a noble goal, we must not be naïve about Islamic ultimate goals (Backtalk: "Obama's Islam Strategy," October). Yes, most Muslims are good neighbors and want peace, but Christopher Ruddy's commentary does not factor in Shariah, to which even peace-loving Muslims are subject. In fact, these ordinary adherents will often join the draconian punishments of stoning, beheadings, amputation of limbs, etc. The only real peace will come when

enough individuals are turned from Muhammad's demonstrably violent religion to more genuinely peaceful faiths such as Christianity.

Eleanor Gustafson
Haverhill, Mass.

This DUMB AMERICAN does not believe
I will live long enough to see Muslims
turn to Christianity here In the U.S.A. since
they are already trying to make their religion
Law here and trying to do away with
the American Law.

Woman cites experience in anti-radical speeches

> She warns that Muslims pose a danger.

By **Laurie Goodstein**
The New York Times

FORT WORTH — Brigitte Gabriel bounced to the stage at a Tea Party convention last fall.

She greeted the crowd with a loud Texas "Yee-HAW," then launched into the gripping personal story she has told in hundreds of churches, synagogues and conference rooms across the United States.

As a child growing up a Maronite Christian in war-torn southern Lebanon in the 1970s, Gabriel said, she had been left lying injured in rubble after Muslims mercilessly bombed her village.

She found refuge in Israel and then moved to the United States, only to find that the Islamic radicals who had terrorized her in Lebanon, she said, were now bent on taking over America.

Brigitte Gabriel, a Lebanese author and speaker, visited Fort Worth in September.
The New York Times

"America has been infiltrated on all levels by radicals who wish to harm America," she said. "They have infiltrated us at the CIA, at the FBI, at the Pentagon, at the State Department. They are being radicalized in radical mosques in our cities and communities within the United States."

Through her books, media appearances and speeches, and her organization, ACT! for America, Gabriel has become one of the most visible personalities who warn that Muslims pose a danger within U.S. borders.

Rep. Peter King, R-N.Y., will conduct hearings Thursday in Washington on a similar theme: that the U.S. is infiltrated by Muslim radicals.

King was the first guest last month on a new cable television show that Gabriel co-hosts with Guy Rodgers, the executive director of ACT! and a Republican consultant who helped build the Christian Coalition, once the most potent political organization on the Christian right.

Gabriel, who uses a pseudonym, casts ACT! as a nonpartisan national security organization.

Yet the organization draws on three rather religious and partisan streams in American politics: evangelical Christian conservatives, right-wing defenders of Israel (both Jews and Christians) and Tea Party Republicans.

Gabriel is only one voice in a growing circuit that includes counter-Islam speakers such as Pamela Geller, Robert Spencer and Walid Shoebat.

What distinguishes Gabriel from her counterparts is that she has built a national grassroots organization.

Gabriel and Rodgers declined to be interviewed in person or by telephone but agreed to respond to questions by e-mail.

Gabriel says she is motivated not by fear or hatred of Islam but by love for her adopted country.

"I lost Lebanon, my country of birth, to radical Islam," she wrote. "I do not want to lose my adopted country America."

In Fort Worth, Gabriel spent nearly an hour after her speech signing books and posing for pictures.

U.S. can't account for its Afghan spending before 2007

By Marisa Taylor
McClatchy Newspapers

WASHINGTON – The U.S. government knows it's awarded nearly $18 billion in contracts for rebuilding Afghanistan over the last three years, but it can't account for spending before 2007.

Thousands of firms received wartime contracts, but the special inspector general for Afghanistan reconstruction found it too difficult to untangle how billions of additional dollars had been spent because of the U.S. agencies' poor recordkeeping.

"Navigating the confusing labyrinth of government contracting is difficult, at best," the inspector general says in a report that was released Wednesday.

The finding raises doubts about whether the U.S. government ever will determine whether taxpayers' money was spent wisely in Afghanistan.

Overall, the U.S. has set aside about $55 billion for rebuilding Afghanistan, but that includes agencies' budget for staff salaries, operations and security.

The Special Inspector General for Afghanistan Reconstruction couldn't parse how much was spent on contractors alone.

SIGAR recommended that the Pentagon, the State Department and the U.S. Agency for International Development create one database to track wartime contracts.

As it stands, the Pentagon has four contracting agencies that oversee contracts, but none of them is sharing information.

BUT, The U. S. Government sure can account for

the U.S. Citizens money we make and spend. Thanks

To our GOOD PRESIDENT AND CONGRESS.

G-20 fallout: Trade barriers more likely

▶ The countries left their summit without any meaningful agreement.

By Paul Wiseman
The Associated Press

WASHINGTON — The world's most important economies are going home to look after themselves.

They left their summit without any meaningful agreement, finding it ever harder to cooperate and more likely to erect trade barriers to protect their own interests.

The Group of 20 meeting of leading rich and developing nations ended Friday in South Korea with no solutions to long-standing tensions over trade and currency, and with the cooperation of the 2008 financial crisis now a distant memory.

The United States couldn't persuade other countries to pressure China to stop manipulating its currency or to limit their own trade surpluses and deficits. The Americans faced charges of currency manipulation of their own by pumping $600 billion into their economy.

The stalemate in Seoul means that trade disputes could intensify, warns Eswar Prasad, professor of trade policy at Cornell University. He's worried that there "may be more open conflicts on currency matters. This has the potential to feed into more explicit forms of protectionism, which could set back the global recovery."

The summit was a diplomatic setback for the United States.

China was supposed to be the villain of the G-20 meeting.

The U.S. and other countries have accused Beijing of keeping its currency, the yuan, artificially low to give its exporters an unfair advantage. The currency manipulation helps Chinese exporters by making their goods cost less around the world, leading to charges that cheap Chinese products cost America jobs at a time when U.S. unemployment is stuck at 9.6 percent.

The U.S. wanted to rally other G-20 delegates to strong-arm China over the yuan. A stronger yuan would reduce the U.S. trade deficit with China, which is on track to match the

More on G-20, 3C

President Barack Obama and South Korean President Lee Myung Bak. Their two nations did not close a free-trade agreement.
The Associated Press/Pablo Martinez Monsivais

Well, We know for sure now, The U.S. is not in the Drivers Seat any more. AND Germany has told the U.S. that the U.S. will not attack any other country unless the U.S. is Attacked first.

G-20

Continued from 1C

At the summit, the U.S. was accused of rigging the currency market.
The Associated Press/Pablo Martinez Monsivais

2008 record of $268 billion.

But the U.S. argument was undercut by accusations that the Federal Reserve was rigging the currency market itself.

Last week, the Fed said it would essentially print $600 billion to jolt the U.S. economy back to life. The U.S. central bank says its plan to buy Treasury bonds was designed to lower long-term interest rates, spur economic growth and create jobs. Since the Fed hinted at the policy in late August, the Dow Jones industrials have risen 13 percent while interest rates on 30-year fixed-rate mortgages have hit a record low of 4.17 percent.

But foreigners saw a more sinister intent: to flood world markets with dollars, driving down the value of the U.S. currency and giving American exporters a price edge.

"Basically, what happened was a diplomatic coup for China," says William Cline, senior fellow with the Peterson Institute for International Economics. A few months ago, countries from Brazil to Germany were criticizing Chinese trade policies. "Fast-forward, and now China and Germany and Brazil are blaming the United States for causing currency problems."

Emerging economies also complained that the Fed's bond purchases would push Treasury yields so low that investors seeking higher returns will overwhelm their fragile markets. The fear: Investors would sink money into emerging market assets — currencies, stocks and other investments. That would push up their currencies, hurt their exporters, trigger inflation, create bubbles in stocks and other assets, and leave them vulnerable to a crash when investors withdraw their money.

The final G-20 statement Friday endorsed the idea that emerging markets can protect themselves from the threat of such "hot money" by imposing controls on the flow of capital — a measure that used to be considered "a big no-no" and a violation of free-trade principles,

says Homi Kharas, a senior fellow at the Brookings Institution. The trend is already starting. China and Taiwan this week announced new capital controls.

The fear is that countries will take even stronger steps to give themselves an advantage, creating the risk of a currency or trade war. The U.S. House has already passed legislation that would let the U.S. government impose punitive tariffs on Chinese imports in retaliation for the weak yuan, though the Senate has not followed.

Cornell's Prasad expects to see China and other countries impose tariffs and duties, subsidize their exporters with cheap bank financing or tax credits, bring cases against each in the World Trade Organization and use bogus health concerns to block some imports.

In a sign of the United States' diminished clout at the summit, the U.S. could not even close a long-awaited free-trade agreement with close ally and summit host South Korea. The trade pact would slash tariffs and other trade barriers between the two countries.

As the G-20 meeting closed, President Barack Obama and many other leaders flew to Japan for the Asia-Pacific Economic Cooperation summit in Yokohama today and Sunday.

At the height of the financial crisis in 2008 and 2009, the G-20 nations tried to present a united front, agreeing to take steps to boost their economies, to reform their financial systems and to reject protectionist policies.

But now that the world economy is growing again — and China and other emerging markets are booming — "that unity has begun to dissolve," Prasad says. "The group is now splintering with competitive policies taking the place of coordinated policy actions." The result: "a situation ripe for conflict," he added.

The G-20 itself acknowledged the problem in its final statement: "Uneven growth and widening imbalances are fueling the temptation to diverge from global solutions into uncoordinated actions."

But the go-it-alone approach, the statement concluded, "will only lead to worse outcomes for all."

76

Monkeys Getting High on Your Dime

Stimulus spending foots the bill for about 50 projects on primates' bad behavior.

By Mattie Corrao

THIS SHOULD MAKE YOU GO APE. Take a hard look at the federal government's "stimulus" spending and you'll find that monkeys are benefiting more than the humans who are footing the bill.

In one of the cases, $71,623 in Recovery Act money funneled to Wake Forest University in Winston-Salem, N.C., was destined to hook monkeys on cocaine.

"When asked how studying drug-crazed primates would improve the national economy, a Wake Forest University Medical School representative said, 'It's actually the continuation of a job that might not still be there if it hadn't been for the stimulus funding,'" says a study that Republican Sens. Tom Coburn of Oklahoma and John McCain of Arizona released. "And it's a good job," the spokesman added. 'It's also very worthwhile research."

In fact, roughly 50 "stimulus" projects deal with monkeys. Nearly $700,000 was appropriated to the Georgia State University Research Foundation to study primate reactions to inequity and unfairness, even though the researchers getting the money acknowledged that the analogous human psychology they were analyzing was already well understood. In the project description, the researchers admit. "Decades of research in economics and social psychology shows that people respond negatively to receiving worse outcomes as compared to other individuals." With little oversight, Congress handed wads of cash over to agencies such as the National Science Foundation, allowing for a grab bag of special projects that have done very little to spur economic growth.

Small wonder that 68 percent of voters believe the "stimulus" has been a total waste. While Americans are struggling to feed their families and find work, monkeys are getting high on their dime. □

Mattie Corrao is executive director of the Center for Fiscal Accountability.

The above shows just how far Congress will go so as to not help out Us Dumb American and what they think of Us Dumb Americans who have lost their homes, jobs and are now on Welfare. This will go on forever if we continue to vote the same ones back into office so they can line their own pockets.

Inquiry targets alleged bid to sway lawmakers

> A "psychological" campaign sought backing for the Afghan war.

By Thom Shanker
The New York Times

WASHINGTON — The American commander in Afghanistan will order an investigation into accusations that military personnel deployed to win Afghan hearts and minds were instructed over their own objections to carry out "psychological operations" to help persuade visiting members of Congress to increase support for the training mission there, military officials said Thursday.

A brief statement issued by the military headquarters in Kabul said Gen. David Petraeus, the commander in Afghanistan, will order an investigation.

The move was prompted by an article released online Thursday by *Rolling Stone* magazine that described an "information operation" or "psychological operation" ordered by Lt. Gen. William Caldwell, who is in charge of training Afghan security forces.

The article said Caldwell and his senior aides ordered a team of specialists to gather information about distinguished visitors and create a campaign to sway traveling American lawmakers to endorse more money and troops for the war.

When the officer running the team resisted, he was ordered in writing to make this his priority. Under pressure, the article said, quoting the officer and documents, the team gathered biographies and things like the guests' voting records — a standard task for headquarters staff before visits by congressional delegations. The article quotes a spokesman in Kabul denying that the command used an information operations cell to influence visitors.

Another *Rolling Stone* article by the same writer, Michael Hastings, led to the forced retirement of Gen. Stanley McChrystal, who was commander in Afghanistan.

Among those said to have been targets of the psychological operation was Sen. Carl Levin, D-Mich., chairman of the Senate Armed Services Committee. Pentagon press secretary Geoff Morrell said Defense Secretary Robert Gates thinks it is important to determine the facts before drawing any conclusions.

Smart kids go to the U.S. Air Force, Army and Navy Academy. And become Officers in the military, they are suppose to be honest Smart Officers and the elite. So tell me what are these Military Schools teaching our young men?

It seems General Petraeus and Defense Sect. Gates wants to cover this up, When Gates talks about he wants to reduce spending and Military personal.

The above article shows and proves that those Educated Idiots in Washington are more of an Idiot than just an Educate smart man, this would not have happen if the U.S.A. had tended to business at home instead of sticking its noise in other countries business, But US DUMB AMERICANS just keep voting those Educated Idiots back into office.

"SEE TWO EXAMPLES BELOW"

How our great leaders in WASHINGTON are turning more AMERICAN CITIZEN into Poverty with their Idiot Laws, Why? Because Us Dumb Americans keep voting the Old Ones back into office.

Why does a retired American that receives a Social Security Check and a small Railroad Retirement check have the Amount of the Railroad check deducted From their S.S. check? He worked and earned each.

Legislation aims to end widows' tax

By Kimberly Hefling
The Associated Press

WASHINGTON — Tens of thousands of the nation's war widows find it perplexing and downright disrespectful to their late military husbands: To fully collect on insurance their husbands bought for them, they must marry another man.

In addition, the widows must remarry when they are 57 or older. Those who remarry earlier miss out, as do widows who never remarry.

At the heart of the issue is a policy known as the "widows' tax."

It says a military spouse whose loved one dies from a service-related cause can't collect both survivor's benefits and the full annuity benefits from insurance the couple bought from the Defense Department at retirement. Instead, the amount of the annuity payment is reduced by the amount of the monthly survivor benefit.

Time after time, members of Congress have promised to help the 55,000 affected widows, but laws enacted to help them have only created a more complicated system.

So what's remarriage got to do with it? Very little, as it turns out. The marriage condition was stuck into the law by Congress as it tried to help the survivors retain certain benefits if they remarried late in life, as is the case with other federal annuities. Because Congress hasn't been able to come up with the money to help all the widows, relief has been limited to that group. The result is an all but incomprehensible mess.

"I've never even wanted to date, much less remarry," said Nichole Haycock, a mother of three teenagers in Lawton, Okla., whose 38-year-old military husband died in 2002. "I already married the love of my life. Why would you bring that as a factor?"

Sen. Bill Nelson, D-Fla., and 10 other senators filed legislation last week to help the widows.

"This has always been an issue of the military doing the right thing and living up to its promises," Nelson said in a statement.

ONE LAST NOTE

Can anyone tell me why our President and Congress are so HELL Bent on giving other countries our money instead of helping the American citizens first who are with out jobs and having to use up their savings and losing their homes?

WHY? Because us DUMB AMERICANS vote the same ones back into office who only think of how to fill their own pockets and receive Kick-Back from countries they voted to give money to, And they let Corp.-Gas Co's-Insurance Co's go up on the price of their product putting more hurt on the American Citizen.

This DUMB AMERICAN thinks congress should help the American Citizens first than help other countries.

ARE WE AMERICANS OR ARE WE IDIOTS?

Government promises cradle-to-grave sustenance yet never delivers. Why do people think it'll be different this time?

Mom and Dad Save the World is the name of a 1992 movie in which a married couple from Earth is transported to a planet of idiots run by a maniacal emperor who's also an idiot. The problems they face in trying to escape are exacerbated because the planet's inhabitants are either too stupid to realize they're stupid, or they know they're dumb and can't figure out what to do about it.

In one scene, an entire army is defeated by a solitary "light grenade" that causes anyone picking it up to vanish. Everyone knows that's what it does, but can't resist picking it up because the words "Pick Me Up" are engraved on it.

That brings to mind the legislation that's coming out of Washington these days that proposes to provide cradle-to-grave sustenance for every man, woman and child inhabiting these shores, regardless of race, creed or legal status. Disregard the fact that we know from history that no government — including France — has ever delivered on such promises. Like the idiots in the movie, we're willing to pick up the light grenade one more time thinking the next result will somehow be different.

For an example of the light-grenade effect, you needn't look far. This newspaper recently reported that Texas should receive close to $4 billion in stimulus money that primarily will maintain a status quo of services by offsetting budgetary shortfalls while producing virtually none of the much-ballyhooed jobs that the nearly $1 trillion bailout bill was designed to create or preserve.

It makes one wonder where and when this spending frenzy will end. When will hard-working citizens look around and realize that enough others are equally fed up that their <u>combined voices</u> will be loud enough to be heard all across this land when they yell, "Enough!"

Enough siphoning money from the pockets of citizens who play by the rules, pay their bills, plan ahead and work hard just so government can support those who will forever have their hands out.

Enough of government granting rights unto itself that aren't in the Constitution and are in opposition to the ones that we possess by virtue of divine endowment, not because some politician decided to let us have them.

Enough trying the fill the shallow end of the pool with water from the deep end. The only way for everyone to swim is if we all swim together.

Enough of government trying to tell us how to care for our families. It's time for government to get its boot off our necks and let us keep enough of our own resources so we can care for ourselves. And that goes for our neighbors, too. Let's let warm-hearted American men and women care for their fellow citizens in need, not some inefficient, faceless bureaucracy thousands of miles from home.

Enough of government rewarding failure. Let's encourage accomplishment instead of punishing it. Let's learn from history that human imagination oftentimes reaches beyond the ability to pay. Sometimes you just have to say "no" to more spending programs.

Let's remind government that we aren't its children and that it's not its money anyway. Let's elect officials who believe in the power of American commerce and ingenuity to create prosperity and not in the power of government to tax us into it.

Let's stop picking up the light grenade of broken promises and misguided government programs and tell government once and for all, "No!" The time is now.

Mom and Dad, please save the world!

ROY SHOCKEY OF KELLER IS A MEMBER OF THE *STAR-TELEGRAM'S* 2009 COMMUNITY COLUMNIST PANEL. ROYSHOCKEY@AOL.COM

I agree 100%
a Pope

Obama: Seniors' checks at risk

❯ Both sides are ready to play the blame game if the U.S. defaults on debt.

By Christi Parsons and Lisa Mascaro
Tribune Washington Bureau

Obama

McConnell

WASHINGTON — President Barack Obama said that he "cannot guarantee" that millions of Social Security beneficiaries will get their checks as scheduled next month unless he and congressional leaders agree to raise the nation's debt limit by Aug. 2, a warning that came as both sides ratcheted up the tension over the monthlong standoff over the debt.

Amid a volley of charges and countercharges over who would bear responsibility for a crisis, the Senate's Republican leader proposed a complex new plan under which Congress would largely surrender its authority to determine the debt ceiling.

The plan, offered by Sen. Mitch McConnell, R-Ky., would force Obama to repeatedly ask for additional debt, which could be politically advantageous to the Republicans but would essentially abandon the GOP quest to use the debt ceiling as a mechanism to force deep cuts in the federal budget. Conservatives widely criticized the plan.

The proposal appeared to be an attempt by McConnell to allow for an increase in the debt ceiling and to avoid the risk of default while putting the entire political onus on the president and on Democratic lawmakers who support his requests.

Their votes in favor of expanding the nation's debt could make for potent election-year political imagery.

McConnell's proposal quickly divided conservatives on and off Capitol Hill. Critics called it an abdication of Congress' responsibility, and Freedom Works, the large Tea Party group, urged its Twitter followers to tell McConnell to "find his spine."

Obama has rejected plans for a short-term agreement, but the White House said McConnell's proposal is an acknowledgment of the importance of meeting U.S. obligations.

The back-and-forth played out in a darkening atmosphere.

The White House said federal officials will face a "Sophie's choice" in deciding what to pay for when federal revenue falls short of bills coming due, as is expected in the absence of an increase in borrowing authority from Congress.

Obama wants a resolution within 10 days to avoid the beginning of unpredictable reactions by financial markets to the growing uncertainty, but Republicans accuse the White House of trying to stampede them to an agreement.

Until now, administration officials have declined to specify which bills they would pay after Aug. 3 with no increase in borrowing authority.

But in an interview with *CBS Evening News*, Obama issued his most explicit warning yet about government benefits and said for the first time that the elderly might not be the only ones affected.

"This is not just a matter of Social Security checks," Obama said. "These are veterans' checks, these are folks on disability and their checks. There are about 70 million checks that go out every month."

Based on cash flow projections, the government will have enough to cover slightly more than 55 percent of its bills in August.

Some Republicans said Obama is resorting to scare tactics to win an increase in the debt ceiling.

"Telling seniors that they may not receive their Social Security checks is his backdoor way of trying to fulfill his desire to raise the debt limit without any conditions," said freshman Rep. Tim Huelskamp, R-Kan.

"US DUMB AMERICANS" can rest easy knowing the Republicans and Democrats, Senators and Congressmen will receive their paycheck so they can keep voting against each other suggestions, That is why "US DUMB AMERICANS" keep voting the same ones back into office, so they get can keep us little old "DUMB AMERICANS" scarred as each year rolls around, One year they have the solution that will last for 15 to 20 years and the next year they do not.

HOW GREAT IT IS TO HAVE OUR GREAT LEADERS ACT LIKE 10 YEAR OLD CHILDREN.

C. L. Pope

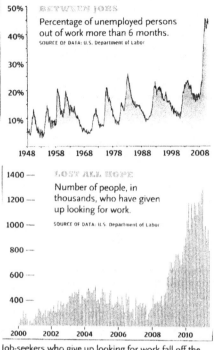

BETWEEN JOBS

Percentage of unemployed persons
out of work more than 6 months.

SOURCE OF DATA: U.S. Department of Labor

50%

40%

30%

20%

10%

1948   1958   1968   1978   1988   1998   2008

1400 —

1200 —

1000 —

800 —

600 —

400 —

LOST ALL HOPE

Number of people, in
thousands, who have given
up looking for work.

SOURCE OF DATA: U.S. Department of Labor

2000   2002   2004   2006   2008   2010

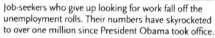

Job-seekers who give up looking for work fall off the
unemployment rolls. Their numbers have skyrocketed
to over one million since President Obama took office.

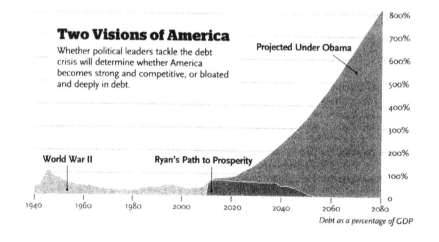

Two Visions of America

Whether political leaders tackle the debt
crisis will determine whether America
becomes strong and competitive, or bloated
and deeply in debt.

Projected Under Obama

World War II

Ryan's Path to Prosperity

800%

700%

600%

500%

400%

300%

200%

100%

0

1940   1960   1980   2000   2020   2040   2060   2080

Debt as a percentage of GDP

Raise the limit

Congress could simply vote to raise the debt ceiling again. It has done so many times before -- 72 times since 1962 and 10 in the past decade -- usually with little drama. But these are not drama-free days in Congress.

Federal debt has nearly doubled since 2004, with huge bills for Social Security and Medicare looming. Tea Party-inspired Republicans have made cutting government spending the focus of their platform and see the debt ceiling debate as a way to force the issue. The White House agrees that now is the time to cut spending but says some new taxes need to be in the mix as well.

Few in Washington or Wall Street think the federal government can simply go on borrowing forever. Debt payments will chew up a bigger and bigger chunk of the budget. Foreign central banks could decide there's a smarter place to park their money. The federal trust funds that now own more than one-third of the debt will dry up. And all the bills will come due someday. When they do, it will be painful. Just look at Greece.

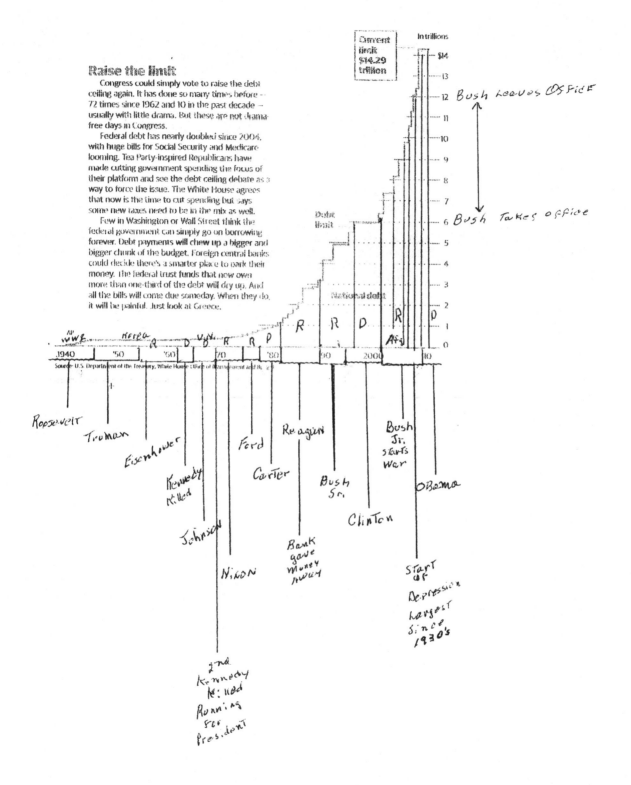

Current limit $14.29 trillion

In trillions

Bush Leaves Office

Bush Takes Office

Debt limit

National debt

Source: U.S. Department of the Treasury, White House Office of Management and Budget

Roosevelt

Truman

Eisenhower

Kennedy Killed

Johnson

Nixon

Ford

Carter

Bank gave money away

Reagan

Bush Sr.

Clinton

Bush Jr. starts war

Obama

Start of Depression Largest Since 1930's

2nd Kennedy Killed Running for President

Our $1 Trillion Nest -Egg Nightmare

THE NATION'S PERSISTENT ECONOMIC downturn has seen many American workers suffer lost jobs, salary cuts, and lost benefits. But even as the recession rages, the states continued to make bold promises to their public-sector employees to perpetuate lavish pension plans and comprehensive healthcare coverage for retirees.

Those promises now have the states in a $1.26 trillion hole — the gap between what must be paid and what has been set aside in public coffers to fund it. According to a recent Pew Center report, "The Widening Gap:

The Great Recession's Impact on State Pension and Retiree Health Care Costs," pension funding shortfalls account for $660 billion of the gap. Unfunded retiree healthcare costs accounted for the remaining $607 billion.

By 2009, states had only about $31 billion, or 5 percent, saved toward their obligations for retiree healthcare benefits. State pension plans were 78 percent funded, declining from 84 percent the year before.

Newsmax reviewed the troubling pension numbers, providing an analysis of how the states got so far behind, and a look at just how deep they'll need to dig to recover from the trillion-dollar mess. □

STATES FEEL PENSION PAIN

The share of state general funds used to pay pensions is growing, reaching 5.3% in 2008. But it would have required nearly 10% to fully fund the liabilities.

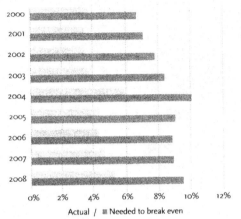

Actual / ■ Needed to break even

SOURCE: U.S. Census Bureau; Moody's Analytics

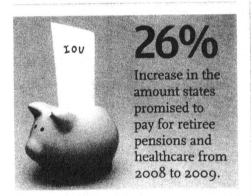

26%

Increase in the amount states promised to pay for retiree pensions and healthcare from 2008 to 2009.

IOU

WALL ST. MADE IT WORSE

Faltering stocks exacerbated pension shortfalls, but funding levels were already dropping even as the market was holding steady in 2006.

▨ S&P 500 Index / ▨ Average Pension Liability Funded

SOURCE: Standard & Poor's; NASRA

CONTRIBUTIONS NOT NEARLY ENOUGH

Since 1993, pension contributions have risen 133% but the gap between contributions and payments continues to widen.

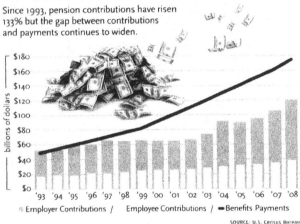

▨ Employer Contributions / Employee Contributions / ━Benefits Payments

SOURCE: U.S. Census Bureau

A WIDENING GAP

Minimum percentage the Government Accountability Office (GAO) recommends funding state health and pension funds is 80%.

▶ States that fell below 80% for fiscal year **2008**: **22**

▶ In **2009**, it expanded to: **31**

87

MARKET RELIANCE

Revenue sources for state pensions trusts show
heavy reliance on investment returns.

SOURCE: Center on Budget and Policy Priorities

27% Employer Contributions

60% Investment Earnings

13% Employee Contributions

PROMISES, PROMISES . . . BUT WHO'S GOING TO PAY?

Despite the recession and a historical drop in investment values, states continue to promise
generous pension and health benefits to retirees. The IOUs now exceed $1.25 trillion dollars.

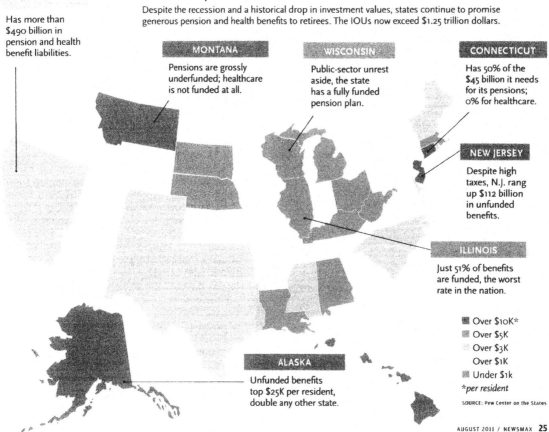

Has more than
$490 billion in
pension and health
benefit liabilities.

MONTANA
Pensions are grossly
underfunded; healthcare
is not funded at all.

WISCONSIN
Public-sector unrest
aside, the state
has a fully funded
pension plan.

CONNECTICUT
Has 50% of the
$45 billion it needs
for its pensions;
0% for healthcare.

NEW JERSEY
Despite high
taxes, N.J. rang
up $112 billion
in unfunded
benefits.

ILLINOIS
Just 51% of benefits
are funded, the worst
rate in the nation.

ALASKA
Unfunded benefits
top $25K per resident,
double any other state.

■ Over $10K*
▨ Over $5K
▦ Over $3K
  Over $1K
▨ Under $1k
*per resident

SOURCE: Pew Center on the States

No free lunch

We have many options for dealing with our national debt, and all of them are painful

By Tim Logan St. Louis Post-Dispatch

The federal government is about to max out its credit card. The Treasury is fast approaching the $14.3 trillion limit on how much it can borrow.

That limit is set by Congress. But this year the Republican-led House of Representatives refuses to raise it, at least not without massive spending cuts. Fine, says President Barack Obama, but not without tax increases. If nothing changes, come Aug. 2, something unprecedented will happen: The

government of the United States will run out of money. It will have to either cut spending nearly in half — overnight — or default on Treasury bonds. Either scenario, say bankers and economists, would have such a devastating effect on the economy that Congress and the White House simply can't let it happen. But despite near-daily talks, the two sides, at least publicly, still seem far from a deal. And Aug. 2 is getting closer. So what would happen? What would it mean if the U.S. Treasury defaults?

A history

No one knows what will happen if the United States issuer of the world's reserve currency, defaults on its debt. But nations have been overextending their credit for quite a long time.

Sovereign debt defaults were first reported in the 4th century B.C., when 10 Greek city-states couldn't make their payments. More recently, defaults have happened every few years, particularly in developing countries. Most of the world's major economies have never defaulted — the exceptions being Germany in 1932 and Russia in 1998.

Defaults of the last 20 years:

1994 A rapid loss in the value of the peso led Mexico to the brink of default. The country couldn't find buyers to refinance its debt, and it needed big loans from the U.S. and International Monetary Fund to bail out its currency.

1997 Boom times in Southeast Asia turned to bust as Indonesia, South Korea, Thailand and others caught the "Asian flu" when local currencies collapsed under heavy debt. The crisis spread quickly but ended quickly, too.

1998 In part because of the Asian crisis, Russia defaulted on $72 billion in debt, setting off economic and political turmoil. Banks failed, strikes were widespread and food prices doubled.

2001 After battling high inflation for a decade, Argentina defaulted on much of its public debt, and its lenders took massive losses. The value of the peso plunged, and the economy took years to recover.

2010 Debt levels soared in Greece during the recession, and the country was forced into huge spending cuts in exchange for European Union and IMF loans to avoid a Euro-threatening default. Ireland, Portugal and now Italy face similar circumstances.

Who owns our debt?

$14.3 trillion

$6 trillion
U.S. government trust funds, mostly Social Security

$4.5 trillion
Foreign central banks and overseas investors, including the United Kingdom, Japan, China and Hong Kong*

$3.8 trillion
U.S. residents and institutional investors

*China and Hong Kong own $1.3 trillion

Source: Government Accounting Office

90

Stage One: The budget chain saw

If the Treasury hopes to avoid default without raising the debt ceiling, it will have to spend less — much less. The government is due to receive roughly $173 billion in tax revenue in August, according to the Bipartisan Policy Center. Yet the federal budget for the month is $307 billion. That's everything from Social Security checks to military salaries to food stamps, and $29 billion in interest payments on Treasury bonds.

As long as it makes those interest payments, the government would stay out of default. But it would have to cut all other spending by 44 percent — forcing some extremely hard choices. Do you pay doctor's bills or food stamps? Do you tell Boeing to float its bills for a month? Do you furlough every federal employee? And there's no way you pay tax refunds.

In a recent study, the Bipartisan Policy Center laid out a few scenarios for how this juggling might work. Here are two of them:

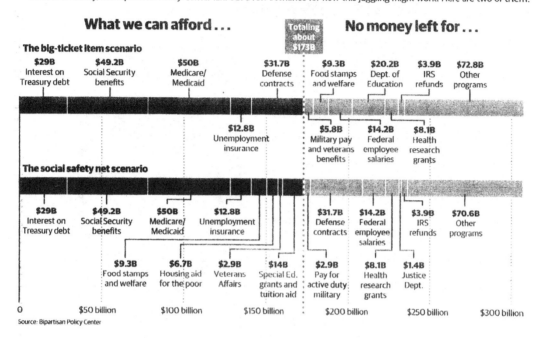

What we can afford . . . Totaling about $173B **No money left for . . .**

Source: Bipartisan Policy Center

Stage Two: Inevitable default

Even sharp spending cuts would require constantly refinancing existing federal debt — likely at higher interest rates. And if one of those rollovers didn't pan out, or the Treasury missed a payment, the government would default on its bonds.

This has never happened, so no one knows how investors would react. But experts predict that it would send a wave of turmoil through the markets. Here are a few potential scenarios:
■ Credit rating agencies downgrade U.S. Treasury bonds (if they haven't already).
■ A rate hike on government debt of at least 0.5 percent, predicts JPMorgan Chase, which would drive up the nation's borrowing costs by $75 billion a year.
■ A downgrade of federal bonds could also drive up borrowing costs for institutions that receive a lot of federal

spending, from states to hospitals to universities.
■ Boost the cost of consumer loans, including mortgages, which could send another shudder through an already weak housing market.
■ A stock-market plunge of 6 to 9 percent, predict JPMorgan and Janney Montgomery Scott, wiping out hundreds of billions of dollars in wealth.

Expect the stock market, banks and businesses to respond further, too.

If bond interest rates stay high, the value of stocks and other investments would likely be depressed indefinitely.

Some experts predict that the uncertainty would lead banks to pull back on lending, making it harder for small business to expand, and for consumers to buy a car or house.

Meanwhile, big companies could sit on cash, lay off employees and delay expansions. This, some warn, would drive the economy back into recession.

Even if the debt ceiling is eventually raised, the consequences of default could play out for a long time. Would a first-ever default make the U.S. and the dollar seem like less of a safe investment?

Permanently higher interest rates on Treasury bonds would mean even more of the federal budget goes toward debt payments.

If investors and foreign governments pulled money out of the U.S., the dollar would weaken relative to other currencies, driving up the cost of imports such as gasoline and electronics, and pushing down the value of goods the U.S. sells overseas.

Other ways out?

Constitutional cage match

There are those who say the answer lies in the 14th Amendment of the Constitution. While it's better known for extending the right of citizenship to everyone born here, the 14th Amendment also states that the "validity of the public debt . . . shall not be questioned."

In other words: The government must pay what it owes.

This clause, the argument goes, could be used to supersede the 1917 act of Congress that created the debt limit. The limit wouldn't be raised; it would simply be ignored. The U.S. would operate like most countries, which don't set statutory limits on borrowing, and keep issuing Treasury bonds, though it's not clear who would buy them.

If the Obama administration takes this route, expect the mother of all legal battles, not to mention nasty political fights. But the courts take time — time that all sides could use to craft a deal.

President Barack Obama and House Speaker John Boehner hit a dead-end Friday.

Where U.S. Troops Are Stationed Abroad . . . And What They're Doing

SECURING AMERICA'S FREEDOM AND safeguarding its interests requires a worldwide effort. More than 325,000 of the United States' 1.5 million military members are deployed in 150 other nations around the globe. Their missions are as varied as the countries they serve in.

From drug interdiction flights over the jungles of Peru in South America to civilian outreach efforts in the colorful marketplaces of Djibouti in Africa; from satellite communications outposts in Norway to the lonely, Cold-War remnants of the Distant Early Warning system above Canada's arctic circle. And then, of course, there are the ongoing operations in Iraq and Afghanistan.

Sending our troops abroad to address global conflicts and national interests is hardly a new phenomenon. Since 1950, an average of 23 percent of all U.S. service members have been stationed on foreign soil. As a percentage of total forces, the low point was 13.7 percent in 1995; the high points were 31 percent in 1951 and 1968. Today's overseas contingent of 326,000 is quite a bit smaller than the annual average of 535,540 from 1950 to 2000. Counting actual boots on the ground (or aboard ship), deployments have ranged from a high of 1,082,777 in 1968 to a low of 206,002 in 1999.

America isn't the only nation that sends its soldiers and sailors abroad, but it is by far the most prolific. U.S. global forces dwarf other international deployments such as those of Great Britain, which has 41,000 of its 217,000 active-duty military personnel abroad, and France, which sends 34,000 of its 360,000 military members overseas. Other global deployments include Germany, with 7,551 soldiers abroad; Italy and Russia with 5,000 each; Australia with 4,000; Canada, 2,900; Netherlands, 2,722; and China, 1,981. □

OVERSEAS CONTINGENT

Breakdown of the U.S. service branches serving abroad:

U.S. ARMY	U.S. AIR FORCE	NAVY	Marines
81,946	71,823	121,864	49,893

Total U.S. Forces Stateside: 1,462,761

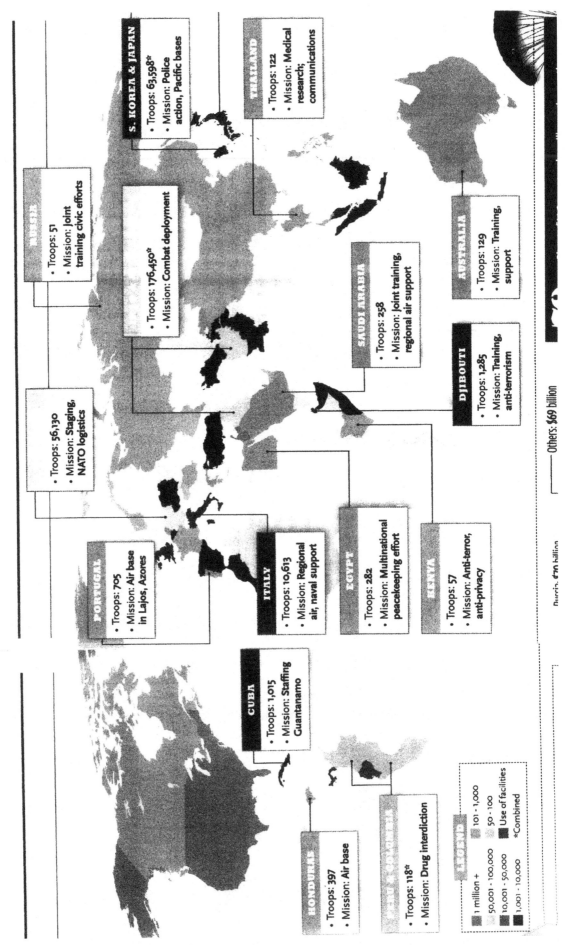

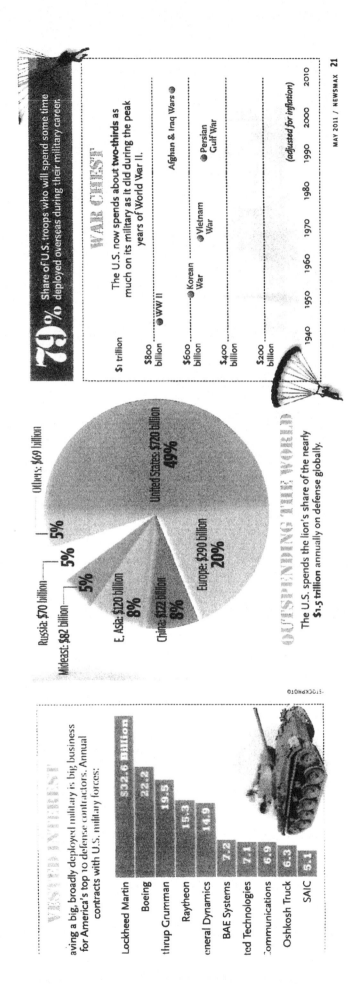

79% Share of U.S. troops who will spend some time deployed overseas during their military career.

WAR CHEST[1]

The U.S. now spends about **two-thirds** as much on its military as it did during the peak years of World War II.

$1 trillion
$800 billion — WW II
$600 billion — Korean War
$400 billion — Vietnam War — Persian Gulf War — Afghan & Iraq Wars
$200 billion

1940 1950 1960 1970 1980 1990 2000 2010

(adjusted for inflation)

OUTSPENDING THE WORLD

The U.S. spends the lion's share of the nearly **$1.5 trillion** annually on defense globally.

- United States: $720 billion — 49%
- Europe: $290 billion — 20%
- China: $122 billion — 8%
- E. Asia: $120 billion — 8%
- Mideast: $82 billion — 5%
- Russia: $70 billion — 5%
- Others: $69 billion — 5%

—STOCKPHOTO

aving a big, broadly deployed military is big business for America's top 10 defense contractors. Annual contracts with U.S. military forces:

- Lockheed Martin: $32.6 billion
- Boeing: 22.2
- thrup Grumman: 19.5
- Raytheon: 15.3
- eneral Dynamics: 14.9
- BAE Systems: 7.2
- ted Technologies: 7.1
- ommunications: 6.9
- Oshkosh Truck: 6.3
- SAIC: 5.1

95

Mission gone askew

Somehow the United States managed to put a man on the moon, fix the Hubble telescope and partner with our former sworn enemies, the Russians, to successfully operate the International Space Station. Those who should have the best interests of the nation as their primary mission — not political party ideology or re-election chances — can't find their way out of a paper bag. It could be humorous, as in the frantic silliness of a Keystone Kops movie, if it weren't so sad and potentially destructive to our nation.

— Susan Spencer, Roanoke

Burgess takes heat for his debt vote

> The North Texas lawmaker doesn't rule out pursuing president's impeachment.

By Aman Batheja
abatheja@star-telegram.com

KELLER — Hours after the Dow Jones industrial average closed down more than 600 points Monday, U.S. Rep. Michael Burgess, R-Lewisville, heard from local conservatives who were unhappy that he supported legislation that many believed led to the calamitous day on Wall Street.

Burgess was one of seven Texas Republicans in the House to vote for the landmark deal that raised the country's debt ceiling by $2 trillion while cutting more than that in public spending.

As Burgess told about 100 people at a NE Tarrant Tea Party meeting, he didn't like the deal but thought supporting it was the right thing to do under the circumstances.

"I came to the conclusion that my country was

U.S. Rep. Michael Burgess spoke to Northeast Tarrant Tea Party members Monday.
Star-Telegram archives

more important than me, and if this meant I wasn't successful in running for re-election, I could not veer into that unknown territory of going past Aug. 2 without a resolution," Burgess said.

Many Tea Party activists view the deal as an instance of Republicans acquiescing too early. When one attendee asked who in the room disagreed with Burgess' decision to support the bill, nearly everyone put a hand in the air.

Mitchell Monis of Keller called the deal "a joke" and told Burgess that he was very disappointed by his decision to support it.

"You caved," Monis said.

Burgess said the recent U.S. debt downgrade by Standard & Poor's made him more certain that supporting the deal was the right thing to do, because the fallout could have been worse.

"I didn't want the country to go through what it is going through right now," Burgess said. "It's not the president's downgrade. The downgrade affected the whole country."

When asked whether he would vote for another increase in the debt limit, Burgess said, "No," adding that he believed both chambers of Congress could instead move forward a balanced-budget amendment.

When one attendee suggested that the House push for impeachment

PoliTex
Find political insights from here to D.C. at
star-telegram.com/blogs

proceedings against President Barack Obama to obstruct the president from pushing his agenda, Burgess was receptive.

"It needs to happen, and I agree with you it would tie things up," Burgess said. "No question about that."

When asked about the comment later, Burgess said he wasn't sure whether the proper charges to bring up articles of impeachment against Obama were there, but he didn't rule out pursuing such a course.

"We need to tie things up," Burgess said. "The longer we allow the damage to continue unchecked, the worse things are going to be for us."

Aman Batheja, 817-390-7695

Burgess has voted with the Republicans 99% of the time against all bills sponsored by the Democrats. So, why should we expect him to vote with the Democrats now.

Tuesday, August 9, 2011

Citizen blowback from debt deal

Americans have a decidedly negative reaction to the debt deal, according to a new McClatchy- Marist poll:

Do you feel things are going in the right direction or in the wrong direction in the country?

Now

Right direction
21%

Wrong direction
70%

Unsure: 10%

January

Right direction
41%

Wrong direction
47%

Unsure: 12%

Did the debate over the debt ceiling give you more or less confidence in Washington?

More
15%

Less
77%

Unsure: 9%

Are you more or less likely to vote for a candidate for Congress in 2012 who supported the deal to raise the debt ceiling?

More likely
36%

Less likely
41%

No difference
11%

Unsure: 12%

BY PARTY ID

	Dem	GOP	Ind
More likely	47%	24%	34%
Less likely	30%	53%	44%
No difference	9%	13%	11%
Unsure	14%	10%	10%

Source: McClatchy-Marist poll of 1,000 adults, Aug. 2-4, 2011; margin of error: +/-3.5 percentage points

MCT

Us Dumb Americans might be upset with Congress now, But Us Dumb Americans will go back to the Polls and vote the same Educated Idiots back into office.

Monday, August 8, 2011

After the disgraceful stalemate in Congress over the debt crisis, there seems to be only one conclusion:

There is no more "government by the people, of the people, for the people" in Washington. There is only "government by the politicians, of the politicians, for the politicians." Only the interest groups — party, ideology, lobbyists, special interests — seem to be heard and heeded.

It appears the "special committee" that will handle the next stage of debt reduction is subject to the

same jockeying for power by the Democratic and Republican parties. This is a sad day for the American people.

— **Velma Stevens, Benbrook**

ALL "US DUMB AMERICANS" have to do is Vote in New Congressman ever 8 years, But we are dumb because we act just like those Educate Idiots in Washington do.

It is "I Said-He Said" so we get what we got. RIGHT ON DUMB AMERICANS.

Lobbies financed 12 on deficit panel

> Supercommittee lawmakers got millions from special interests with a stake in potential cuts.

By Jack Gillum
The Associated Press

WASHINGTON — The 12 lawmakers appointed to a new congressional supercommittee in charge of with tackling the nation's fiscal problems have received millions in contributions from special interests with a direct stake in potential cuts to federal programs, an Associated Press analysis of federal campaign data has found.

The newly appointed members — six Democrats and six Republicans — have received more than $3 million total during the past five years in donations from political committees with ties to defense contractors, healthcare providers and labor unions. That money went to their re-election campaigns, according to AP's review.

Supporters say the lawmakers were picked for their integrity and experience with complicated budget matters. But their appointments have already prompted early concerns from campaign-finance watchdog groups, which urged the lawmakers to stop fundraising and resign from leadership positions in political groups.

The committee, created as part of the debt limit and deficit reduction agreement enacted last week, must cut more than $1 trillion from the budget during the coming decade. If it fails to do so by late November — or if Congress votes down the committee's recommendations — spending triggers would automatically cut billions of dollars from politically delicate areas like Medicare and the Pentagon.

The lawmakers represent a large swath of political ideology and geography, but they have some things in common: They received more than $1 million overall in contributions from the healthcare industry and at least $700,000 from defense companies, the AP found. Those two industries, especially, are sensitive to the outcome of the committee's negotiations because the automatic spending cuts could affect them most directly.

The committee's co-chairmen — Sen. Patty Murray, D-Wash., and Rep. Jeb Hensarling, R-Dallas — each received support from lobbyists and political committees, including those with ties to defense contractors and healthcare lobbyists. Hensarling's re-election committee, received about $11,000 from Lockheed Martin and $8,500 from Northrop Grumman.

After reading the above, Is there any doubt who will decide what is and is not good for US DUMB AMERICANS?

IF I WAS A CONGRESSMAN

1. I would live by the Constitution.
2. I would hire a full time Constitution Attorney to help me.
3. Accept no money from lobbyist. The CEO has to come see me and Lobbyist will not write my bills.
4. If a Republican brings up a bill that is good for all the country I will vote for it. If it is not good for all of the US I will not vote for the bill. Same for the Democrats.
5. I would not vote to tell which college can play in the ChampshipBowl's.
6. I will vote to bring all of our troops home including Peace Keeping Troops and especially the ones on the DMZ Zone in Korea that has been there for 50years.
7. I will not vote to give other countries money so we can tell them how to run their country. And I would not threaten any country unless they start or threaten war on the U.S.
8. Vote to put all of our Federal Agencies and the Military in communication with each other to fight Terrorist here in the US.
9. Send Illegals back home, Put large fines on any company that hires them, and this includes the Muslins that preach even a hint of Preaching or Aiding anyone to commit a Terrorist Act. And closing the Muslim Schools that even hint of teaching children to hate an American.
10. I would vote to bring back to the U.S. Companies that do not pollute the Air-Water-Rivers and cities
11. I would sponsor a bill to fine any company that goes up on the price of their product, This includes Banks-Electric Co's-Cities-States and Taxes when the country is in a Depression.
12, I would vote to put a limit on what Insurance Co's can charge
13. Any country that is attacked by another and ask for help from the U.S. I would vote to help them, IF, they were not the cause of the war.
14. I would vote to lower taxes on the poor and rich.
15. I would vote to fine any School, City or State that passed a bill for a certain project than after the bill was passed, they used the money for other than the project people voted for.
16. Judge's and Schools should hold parents responsible for kids that cause trouble at school and off school grounds by the parents paying a fine.
17. I would vote to have the VA have the best care possible for Vet's and the Military.
18. I would vote for a bill that is good for the US and if it offends another country. 'TO BAD'
19. I am not a Politician, I would just want to be 'Your Respected Congressman'
20. If I was elected, Would Nancy put me way back in the Basement?

Congress' approval rating sinks to all-time low

CALIFORNIA — Just 13 percent of Americans say they approve of the way Congress is doing its job while 83 percent disapprove, the worst disapproval rating for lawmakers in more than 30 years, according to a Gallup Poll released Wednesday. The previous record low approval rating was 14 percent in July 2008, a time of high prices for gasoline and a poor economy. For the year, Congress averaged about a 19 percent approval rating. The poll is based on telephone interviews with 1,019 adults from Friday to Sunday. It has a margin of error of plus or minus 4 percentage points. — Los Angeles Times

And Americans go right back and vote these Idiots right back into office.

Maybe the American Citizens are the ones that are the real Idiots.

MORE AMERICAN THAN AMERICA

By Megan Matteucci

FOREIGN NATIONS THAT USED TO BEG the United States for aid have become showcases for economic vitality. Maybe America, which borrows 41 cents of every dollar it spends, could learn a few lessons from them. These nations have reduced government regulation, slashed corporate taxes, promoted free markets — in short, they've become more American than America.

■ **Japan**'s asset and real estate bubble burst in the 1990s leading to a "lost decade," says Brookings Institution senior fellow Barry Bosworth. What spared the Japanese more pain is they are more frugal that Americans, Bosworth says. "Japanese households don't borrow so much money. I don't think there is another country that borrowed against itself like the U.S. did."

■ **Canada:** Chris Edwards, director of tax policy studies at the Cato Institute tells Newsmax that 15 years ago, Canada was in a desperate debt situation. "The government was spending and borrowing too much. They cut taxes, cut spending and turned a corner." Edwards, a Canada native, adds: "A lot of liberals in the U.S. are saying you can't cut spending because it will be bad for the economy. I think that's nonsense, and Canada proves the case."

■ **Korea and Sweden** repaired their economies by exporting. They allowed exchange rates to plunge making their exports cheaper and more competitive.

■ **Sweden and Germany** struggled in the 1990s, yet both are thriving today. Sweden's banks and real estate crashed, but the government took over the banks and stabilized the economy.

"Germany did not dig itself as big a hole as we did because it was able to convince companies to do a share work program," Bosworth says. "They cut hours instead of laying people off." □

Unemployment in May 2011:

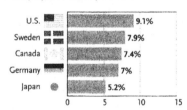

U.S.	9.1%
Sweden	7.9%
Canada	7.4%
Germany	7%
Japan	5.2%

SOURCE: www.tradingeconomics.com

Us Dumb Americans need to vote in a New President and all New Congressmen (Democrats & Republicans) come the next election. But, We will wait and see how many of Us Dumb Americans will vote the same old Congress People back into office.

E. S. Bope

Sept 1, 2011

I GIVE UP

A Republican Congressman goes to Washington just to vote for Bills sponsored by Republicans and to vote against every bill sponsored by the Democrats and vice versa. As an average Dumb American citizen this Dumb American just can not understand this. But, I do know this is another reason why the American public is so discussed with our congress, not one cares about us Dumb Americans. They only bow to the Lobbyist, Oil Co. and the Rich. But, it's the fault of us Dumb Americans that keep sending the same So and So's back to Washington.

The U.S. does not know how to win and end a war and the U.S. should have gotten out of Iraq right after Hussan was killed. But, the U.S. had to stick around and show and tell Iraq how to run their country which was none of our business, Plus getting a lot of our men killed.

The more I write about us DUMB AMERICANS and telling what is wrong with our Great Leaders and country I did not realize just how much trouble our Great Leaders have gotten us into.

So, I am just going to stop here because I do not think there is any hope for the U.S. to change it's ways in my life time. Being 80 years of age. Our great leaders will not listen to the Americans who do and did the fighting for them as our Great Leaders set back and lie and take bribes in their over size stuff chairs with their big cigar smoking up Washington.

I am ready to go to the Back Woods in the mountains where I do not get the newspaper and listen to some Good Old Country Music and enjoy the scenery.

Does any one know of a mountain that is free of Pollution and the river runs clear?

" HEAVEN HELP OUR CHILDREN AND GRANDCHILDREN"

CONCLUSION

IT IS A SHAME THAT THIS DUMB AMERICAN FEELS THIS WAY TOWARD OUR OWN PRESIDENT AND CONGRESS PEOPLE. I KNOW OF NO ONE THAT SUPPORTS THEM, EXCEPT, EACH OTHER.

MY UNCLE FOUGHT IN WW2 AND MY BROTHER AND I SPENT 4 YEARS IN THE NAVY, GOING TO KOREA TWICE, AND WE FOUGHT FOR ALL THIS MESS.???????

Author:
Clifford L. Pope
6925 Sandstone Ct.
Ft. Worth, Tx. 76120
817-451-3842

DOES ANY ONE KNOW WHERE I CAN
FIND A MOUNTAIN WITH CLEAN AIR
AND A RIVER THAT RUNS CLEAR?